WYATT

BROTHERHOOD PROTECTORS WORLD

LEANNE TYLER

Twisted Page Press LLC

BROTHERHOOD PROTECTORS

ORIGINAL SERIES BY ELLE JAMES

Brotherhood Protectors Series

Montana SEAL (#1)

Bride Protector SEAL (#2)

Montana D-Force (#3)

Cowboy D-Force (#4)

Montana Ranger (#5)

Montana Dog Soldier (#6)

Montana SEAL Daddy (#7)

Montana Ranger's Wedding Vow (#8)

Montana SEAL Undercover Daddy (#9)

Cape Cod SEAL Rescue (#10)

Montana SEAL Friendly Fire (#11)

Montana SEAL's Mail-Order Bride (#12)

SEAL Justice (#13)

Ranger Creed (#14)

Delta Force Rescue (#15)

Montana Rescue (Sleeper SEAL)

Hot SEAL Salty Dog (SEALs in Paradise)

Hot SEAL Hawaiian Nights (SEALs in Paradise)

Hot SEAL Bachelor Party (SEALs in Paradise)

To Michael Knight for helping me with the in-depth study of trauma writing and to Kate McKeever for making sure I met my deadline. This book would not have been the same without both of your support.

CHAPTER 1

COLLEEN SUMMERS WALKED into the Pied Piper Bar with her friends Carly and Simone, noticing a group of frat boys crowded around one side of the bar. She could spot their type from any distance after all these years of leaving college behind. They all looked the same with their cocky attitudes, khaki pants, button downs or polo shirts, expensive leather loafers and good looks –even those who weren't but had the pedigree and wealth to make up for it. Seeing them here tonight made her stomach clinch into a knot, but she took a breath and vowed not to let their presence ruin the evening for her or Carly.

Their friend Jules was already seated at a table, kicked back and enjoying a single-malt scotch, waiting on them. Simone made a beeline for the 8x8 stage while Carly headed to the bar. Colleen decided to put some music on at the juke box and selected a few of her favorite songs because she felt like privately celebrating. She'd gotten the call for a second job interview this afternoon and it was all she could do to keep her enthusiasm to herself on the drive over, but she'd managed not to share her secret after picking up her two friends. She didn't want to jinx her new job prospect of working with one of the top event planners in Chicago by talking about it with them before it even happened. Besides, tonight wasn't about her. It was about Carly and her divorce from Justin Porter.

Just remembering his name left a bad taste in Colleen's mouth, but she was certain it was nothing compared to what it left for Carly. Watching Carly struggle to get out of her marriage had made Colleen not want to tie the knot anytime soon and her resolve to stay single stronger. Her parents hadn't been role models promoting the institution nor were her other two friends, Jules and Simone, eager to head down the aisle either.

Biting her bottom lip, Colleen selected a final song, then swayed to the music, before turning around to watch her friends. Simone was shimmying up and down the chrome pole on the stage, trying to draw the attention of the men in the bar like she normally did. But tonight, her red-haired friend was working it a little too hard. Colleen could tell something was up with Simone. She'd been way too quiet in the car ride over, so had Carly which was understandable. They'd practically forced her to come tonight and given her the outfit she was wearing.

"Hit me again." Carly's voice carried from over at the bar as she clunked down an empty shot glass.

"Woohoo, that's the spirit," Simone called. The more she swayed and shimmied the higher her dress rose. Yet, she was still dancing alone.

Jules lounged at the table nursing the single-malt scotch. She was the perfect youth counselor in Colleen's opinion. She wouldn't let any of those kids who frequented the center get away with bull because if it could be done then Jules had done it in her youth and lived to tell about it.

"You guys look like a hair color commercial," Carly laughed.

"Look who's talking." Jules turned in her direction and gestured with her drink. "You're the one who looks like something out of a Victoria's Secret catalog."

Colleen couldn't hear what Carly said in return, but her friend blushed, reached a hand to her shoulder length honey-blonde hair, and smoothed the imaginary flyaway strands back into place. The edges of her lightweight faux leather jacket pulled apart, revealing a white clinging tank top that showed off her flat tummy. The ensemble was finished with matching black short shorts that covered all the essentials and did marvelous things for her legs. As if they weren't long enough, the black studded, open toe, mid-ankle boots she wore added three more inches to her height. Simone had said the outfit had screamed 'take me home tonight', but no one had mentioned that to Carly.

Simone left the pole and danced over to the bar, looking Carly in the eye. "The whole point of this evening is to get you out of your comfort zone. You're the one that wanted a change in your life. We wanted it to be a liberation now that you're officially divorced from that control freak Justin Porter."

Carly downed the next shot of tequila and set the glass back on the bar. "Another one bartender."

"Pace yourself and don't forget to drink water. You don't want to find yourself flat on the floor," Colleen warned, giving her a sweet smile. She rushed over to the bar aware of the frat boys being on the other side watching Carly. Colleen reached for her friend's hand, leading her back to their table to make sure Carly didn't down another shot too quickly.

Simone followed with a pitcher of water and tray containing the next round of drinks. When the next song began to play, Jules finally got to her feet after a little cajoling and danced with her and Simone. All three urged Carly to join them, but she refused, sipping her water instead. To Colleen's dismay a few frat boys joined them on the stage and they danced to the music. A knot of apprehension formed in the pit of her stomach and she tried to push it aside so what if they were dancing with them. Other couples had joined them too. She was being silly to worry about their being there tonight.

When a hard and fast tempo song played, Jules and Simone danced and jumped around. Colleen moved off to the side and took photos of them with her phone, giggling the whole time at their moves and the way they looked goofing off and having a good time. But then the music changed to a slow dance and one of the frat boys approached Simone and started dancing with her. Colleen swayed to the music and watched, unsure she liked the way he was getting into her friend's personal space, but Simone didn't seem to mind. So why should she?

When the music ended, the three headed back to the table and found Carly sitting there as they'd left her.

"What have you been up to?" Simone asked.

"Narrowly escaping the rough hands of the long-haired man at the bar. I think I've had enough shooters for one night."

"We need food." Colleen picked up the small menu on the table and rattled off the appetizers. "Let's get the slider platter and the loaded cheesy bacon fries."

"Girl, just because you can eat like that and not gain an ounce doesn't mean we're all blessed with those genetics," Simone said.

"Live a little." Jules snatched the menu from Colleen. "I'll go order and be right back with a round of beer for us all. Longnecks or a pitcher?"

"Longnecks."

Jules returned a short time later with four bottles

and handed them out. "Let's toast Carly and her new life."

"Here. Here." Colleen raised her bottle.

Carly blushed and tried to hide the fact by drinking her beer.

The waitress came shortly after with the sliders and the fries. The four talked, scarfed down the food, and then it was finally time to shower Carly with the naughty gifts they'd brought. Colleen was especially proud of her offering and she hoped Carly would appreciate her cleverness.

Simone squealed, stomping her feet happily on the floor as she produced a small tiger print gift bag with black tissue paper. "I hope you have lots of fun with these."

Carly actually eyed the bag as if she were afraid to reach inside, but finally she stuck her hand in and pulled out furry, leopard print handcuffs. "Oh…Well… Uh…Yea-."

"This one's from me," Colleen said, sitting down another small, sparkly gift bag with bright tissue paper.

"Is there a theme to these gifts?" Carly asked.

"Yes, that you use them," Simone said.

The girls giggled, but Colleen held her breath as Carly reached inside and pulled out a handful of glow in the dark condom packets. Colleen watched closely as Carly's hand was suspended above the bag for a few seconds before she dropped them back inside and reached for Jules sedate white gift bag with pink tissue.

Maybe my gift had been too over the top after all?

"Do I even want to look inside this one? It looks too innocent which means it's not," Carly pointedly looked at Jules.

Jules shrugged. "Depends on how adventurous you are."

Taking a deep breath, Carly pulled out the pink tissue and unwrapped a biker babe leather thong teddy and whip set. "Good heavens."

No. Mine wasn't. That one was!

Colleen gave a sigh of relief and laughed with her friends as Carly's cheeks flamed and she wrapped the items back in the tissue and stuffed them into the gift bag again. She put the other two gift bags inside of Jules' and then stowed the gifts inside her large black bag.

"You guys didn't have to do this or bring these here…tonight. You could have given them to me at my apartment."

Colleen shook her head. "That place is so small. I swear, my linen closet is bigger."

Simone snorted, made a face, and then covered her nose and mouth with both hands.

"Sorry you don't approve, but it was all I could afford. I wasn't awarded alimony."

"Which is asinine!" Jules stood up. "That is the one thing about your divorce I don't agree with. How could the judge grant it without awarding you alimony? Justin Porter comes from money. Didn't one of his ancestors found that country club he belongs to?"

Carly nodded. "One of the first members. But his family doesn't like to brag."

Simone snorted again. "Is that why he mentioned it so often when you were first dating?"

"Did he?"

"Yes." Jules tossed a used napkin on the table. "He got the house. While you moved into a tiny apartment that you barely can afford without any support. You have no job. Your parents aren't speaking to you because you left him, it's—"

"I have a job interview next week now that everything is settled and I can focus on not going to court every day."

"The legal system is screwy. Where is justice in the world?" Jules continued to fume.

Colleen patted their friend on the shoulder. "It'll be okay. The youth center will find money somewhere to support the programs for the kids. There have been budget cuts before and the center has survived."

Jules kicked the leg of a nearby chair. "Not like these cuts."

"I'm sorry, Jules, I hadn't realized it had gotten so bad this week," Simone said. "Someone should have let me know when I got back in town from my business trip."

Jules shook her head. "Enough about me. It's Carly's

night out and we still have plenty of time before the bar closes. Another round of drinks? A round of pool?"

"A little pole dancing for our divorcee?" Simone suggested, getting to her feet and pulling at Carly's hand, trying to persuade her to get up on the stage. "You're not going to find Mr. Right Now if you stay hidden behind a table all night. You gotta get out on the dance floor and move your moneymaker."

Carly shook her head and held up her hands. "Guys, please, stop. I think I've had more than my limit of alcohol for one night. Dancing when I feel like this won't be good. All I'll attract is a bucket and a mop."

"Okay, then what would you like to do?" Colleen asked, reaching out and taking her hands in hers. "We're here to please."

"I want to spend time with my besties. Is that so wrong? I know you think I need to have a hot night out, but have I drawn a man to me tonight? Well, other than Mr. Longhair tattoo guy, but you know. Have either of you been propositioned? No. Is there something wrong with us?"

"I think we're sending off the wrong vibes," Colleen said. "We're woman, hear us roar, but stand your distance, buster."

Jules smirked. "You got that right."

"More the reason we need to get up on the stage and shake our booties." Simone left the table, went to the juke box and selected *Firefly* and went to the stage and proceeded to sway and gyrate.

Colleen liked the song so she ran to Simone, laughing. They held hands, raising their arms in a slow-motion wave. Soon Jules and Carly joined them. It wasn't long until a few of the guys in the bar sauntered over and began dancing as well.

Colleen continued dancing with Simone and the guys danced around them and with them. Even when a slower song came on, she stayed alone, but that was okay as she swayed to the music by herself. It didn't bother her that not one of the guys had made an offer to ask her for the dance.

When the songs ended, Colleen followed her friends back to their table wondering if she had any beer left to quench her sudden thirst.

A bell rang near the bar and everyone stopped what they were doing. The bartender climbed up on the wooden surface and announced, "Last call of the night. We'll be closing in fifteen."

Wolf howls and cheering came from the group of frat boys and then there was a round of slaps on the backs of some of the guys.

"Wonder what that was all about?" Jules arched a brow. "Well, I hate to bail, but I have an early morning meeting."

"On a Saturday?" Simone questioned.

Jules nodded. "With all the budget cuts we have to figure out how we're going to keep the few programs we can from tanking."

"See you. Call if you need to talk." Colleen made a

sad face before hugging her. When she pulled away she looked at Carly and Simone. "I need to hit the ladies before we leave."

"Okay. We'll wait for you at the bar," Carly told her.

Colleen downed the last of her beer and grabbed her purse before making her way across the bar to the glowing restroom sign. She had to pass by the frat boys, but they were too engrossed in themselves to pay her any attention. She'd had a bad experience with that crowd in college and she didn't want to have a repeat tonight while she was alone and she really needed to get into the ladies.

The hallway leading to the restrooms appeared longer and darker because an overhead light was blown. Then she heard the sound of footsteps behind her. Her heart began to pound. She slowly looked over her shoulder and saw a man go into the men's room and chided herself for being silly and letting the fact those frat boys being here put her on edge all night. She hurried into the one stall women's and locked the door behind.

Her cellphone rang while she was in the stall and she dug in her purse wondering who would call her at such a late hour on a Friday night. It was a voice recording from her pharmacy letting her know her monthly prescription was ready to be picked up, so she mentally added that to her to do list for the next day.

Going over the list while she attended to business she went to wash and dry her hands. Brunch with her divorced parents. A trip to the dry cleaners. The pharmacy and then grocery before home to do laundry and prepare quick meals for the next week. She really lived a rather humdrum life. No wonder she had men lining up to take her out, but maybe that was about to change if she got this new job.

Walking to the door, she slipped the lock out of the latch and the door came flying in on her. A man was upon her instantly, whacking her across the face with the palm of his hand, knocking her backwards. She slammed against the stall wall, banging her head. The metallic taste of blood seeped into her mouth. The man punched her in the stomach. She doubled over in agony with a gasp as the breath whooshed from her parted lips. He grabbed her ponytail and pulled her around, slamming her against the solid plastic wall again with a thud.

Colleen grunted when her cheek banged the cool surface. Stunned and rattled, it took her several moments to gather her wits about her to realize what was happening as the man pinned her hard up against the wall with his body. An all too familiar feeling of being pinned down, held down as her clothes were being ripped from her body flashed through her mind and she closed her eyes tightly, trying to block it from her memory. But as she focused on the present, it was to the horrifying realization that he had pushed her skirt up as far as he could, her panties were down around her ankles, and he'd wedged her legs apart with his knee. She couldn't move because he had her arms trapped in front of her. She tried to scream, but no sound came from her parched throat. She tried again, but only a low, whimper escaped. Paralysis had frozen her, making her almost mute and immobile as he fumbled with his belt and zipper while breathing heavily against the side of her face, biting savagely at her ear. His sharp teeth raked against the soft flesh of her ear lobe.

The thought that he was going to rape her ran through her mind and it made her angry. Why her? She hadn't gotten drunk. She hadn't danced in a way to lead any man on in the bar. Had she? Her mind raced, retracing the night, but confusing images from her past crept in of another night she'd tried to forget from long ago. For a second she was back in college, being pinned down while one fraternity boy took his pleasure with her and two others watched.

The damp smell of the lady's room changed to a musty smell of a frat house basement and her anger mounted until she was able to finally break free of the paralysis that had overcome her. She pushed back to fight this man off finally freeing one arm. He bit her ear hard and groped at her breast. She sneered and jabbed with her right elbow back and upward, catching him in his ribcage. Unfortunately doing little injury to him before he was able to pin her arm again.

A sharp crack and that sounded like a wall exploding was the only thing that caused the man to stop his assault. Where she'd felt something hard on her backside it had wilted like a flower and a wetness was left in its wake. Had he ejaculated on her? The thought made her sick.

He backed away from Colleen, zipped his pants, grabbed her purse off the bathroom floor and ran out the door.

Clinging to the plastic wall of the stall, she didn't move for the longest time even after the bathroom door closed. The paralysis had returned mingled with fear that the man would come back and continue his assault. She wasn't sure when she slowly sank to the floor, crying and trembling so hard that her vision was so blurry a crumpled piece of tissue looked like a plucked carnation. All she knew was she curled up in ball and held her knees to her chest, rocking herself gently, trying to forget what happened, like she'd done after the first time back in college.

CHAPTER 2

TWO BLACK SUV police cruisers charged with lights and sirens blasting through the almost deserted Chicago streets toward the waterfront. They arrived on the scene within minutes, and Wyatt Kincaid stepped from one of the vehicles and led the way as his other team members dressed in black cargo pants and t-shirts like him piled out of the cruisers, stopping a few feet from where a woman argued with a detective who refused her entry into the bar.

"You don't understand. I was in there earlier with my friends. If I hadn't had to leave to catch the 'L', I would have been with them when the shooting happened. I know they're still in there. I need to check to make sure they're okay."

Commander Hawkeye Burns of the Chicago PD came around the side of one of the cruisers and stood beside Brand Chambers, his team leader. "That's Jules

Gentry. One of your men needs to stay with her. As I understand it, she spotted the getaway car. I'll explain to the detective that your man is taking over."

Brand nodded, turned to his men and pointed at Loverboy, the retired Army Ranger.

"McLeod. She's yours. Find out what you can about what she knows and make sure no reporters get near her."

"You got it."

"Donovan, Kincaid, follow me," Brand ordered, leading them into the Pied Piper Bar.

The overhead lights had been raised to full throttle. A few tables and chairs were toppled over. The glass mirror behind the bar was shattered along with many of the bottles of alcohol on display. Uniformed policemen, a few detectives, and the crime scene unit as well as the coroner milled around doing their jobs. A gurney with a black body bag was ready to be rolled outside.

Wyatt stared at the body bag longer than he should have. His airway became constricted and he found it difficult to breathe. It shouldn't bother him to see it. He hadn't seen his Humvee mates that had died in the explosion in Afghanistan carted away in that fashion. It was only the association of the body bag and death that brought on the reaction.

Liam Donovan flicked his arm, drawing his attention to the people huddled together away from the crime scene. Commander Burns had described in the

SUV the women he wanted them to look after. Wyatt spotted the two of them huddled together at a table, heads bent close as they talked to one another. A blonde in a leather jacket, short shorts with long, sexy legs and ankle boots. The other was a redhead in a short dress.

"I'll take the redhead," Donovan said before Brand could issue assignments.

Brand smirked. "Of course, you will. Remember she's an assignment, not your date for the weekend. You will keep your libido in check, Don Juan."

"Hey now, you know I'm not really a lover boy like McLeod. The guys in my unit only nicknamed me that because it went with Donovan."

"But you do have a way with the ladies just the same," Wyatt pointed out.

Donovan punched him in the arm again. "You're not helping, man. You're not helping."

"So, do I get the blonde?" Wyatt asked.

Brand shook his head. "No. She's mine."

Of course, she is, Wyatt thought. That was always the way it went, but there had to be an assignment for him. He looked around and spotted the commander coming toward them.

"Good. I see you've found your assignments so far," Commander Burns said. "The blonde is Carly Manning, the one who used the bat on the shooter. The other is Simone Reid. She had a gun pointed at her, fired, but no bullet. We're not sure if that means the gang has targeted her or not. Kincaid, I understand you're good with PTSD victims."

"That's right, Commander Burns."

"Then come with me. Special Victims was called in. Apparently, we had more than a shooting in this bar tonight. Your assignment is being loaded into an ambulance headed to Chicago Medical Center. I'll get you a ride with them to the hospital. Stay with her and make sure she is treated with the best care. At this point, we're not clear to what extent her injuries range. We aren't even sure if there was penetration. Likewise, we don't know if the incident was random or related to the gang or not. It's your job to find out as much as you can from her as possible without causing more stress than she's already been through."

Wyatt nodded and then made eye contact with Brand. "I'll be in touch."

Brand nodded.

Wyatt followed the commander across the bar and out the opposite side to where the EMT was closing the door on the back of the ambulance.

"Hold up," Burns called. "Do you have room for a ride along?"

The EMT nodded and Wyatt climbed in the back with the other medic who was working, checking the girl out.

"Hi. Where do you want me so I'm out of your way?" he asked.

"Over there." The medic pointed to the built-in seat. "Strap yourself in."

"Is she unconscious from an injury?"

"Shock. We see this in trauma victims." He spread a thin silver blanket over her. "It's my job to keep her warm and comfortable until we get her to the hospital."

"Commander said Special Victims was called in, but you weren't sure if there was penetration."

The EMT looked at him. "We pick them up and transport them. You'll have to ask SV at Chicago Med those questions. She's been beaten."

Wyatt nodded. "So, you think that was her attacker's intent?"

"There were semen stains on the back of her skirt."

Leaning back in the seat, Wyatt shook his head. The poor woman. A busted lip and a black eye were visible evidence of her attack. It was the bruising that no one could see that would take much longer. She went out with her friends to have a good time only to have it end like this in the lady's room. He would have to report this to Brand eventually, but maybe in the morning once he had more news on the woman. It would be good to at least know her name.

The EMT didn't. He'd seen the clipboard paperwork where the man had been writing vital statistics as he'd climbed into the ambulance. They were calling her Jane Doe for now. That must mean she had no identification on her. Had her attacker taken her purse?

Wyatt pulled out his phone and began texting

Brand. His team leader needed to be aware of these facts. Commander Burns needed to get his men on finding the guy who had attacked this woman and get her purse with her wallet back. The man had her vital information. He knew where she lived. He had access to her financial records, any credit cards she carried with her. Keys to her apartment.

Item by item ticked off in Wyatt's brain and he typed faster. His right leg bounced up and down, keeping a rhythmic staccato as he waited for Brand to respond to his message.

Finally, his phone buzzed.

"Colleen Summers. Don't take her home tonight. Even if they release her. Go to a hotel."

"Roger that."

Wyatt leaned forward. "Her name is Colleen Summers."

The EMT looked up. "How'd you find that out?"

"My team leader was talking to her friends at the bar."

"Thanks man. So, what are you?"

"What do you mean?"

"What's your purpose being here in this ambulance, riding to Chicago Med with her?"

"I'm her protector."

CHAPTER 3

CHICAGO MEDICAL CENTER emergency room was hustle and bustle, get out of the way or get run over with a gurney, patient in need coming through the double doors. He was ushered to a room with Colleen to wait in the ER due to the nature of her injuries. Special Victims arrived shortly. He introduced himself to Detectives Shipman and Holliday.

"Commander Burns already explained your position here," Holliday said. Her intense, steel-blue eyes watched him closely as if she still wasn't sure she wanted him there or not, even if he was to protect the victim. "If it's okay with you, we'll run this as a normal SV case until deemed otherwise, keeping you in the know the whole way through. We know the ropes here and how this hospital works."

"What Holliday means is, we've got our connections and can get around hospital red tape when we need to where you can't," Shipman cut in. She had a nice smile and warm brown eyes that complimented her blonde hair.

"Sounds good to me," Wyatt agreed. "Whatever will make my job easier protecting Ms. Summers."

A nurse entered the room. "We can't do a rape kit until she comes around. I suppose you'll be wanting me to hurry that along?"

Holliday nodded. "The EMT said it is shock. Not injury."

"But shock can do damage if mishandled," the nurse advised. "You know that."

"And a rape kit is only viable—"

"Yeah, Yeah, I know, Holliday. We do the same song and dance every time." The nurse went to the cabinet on the wall and punched in a code to unlock the panels, taking out the necessary items. She filled a syringe with something and gave Colleen a shot.

A few seconds later Colleen's head began moving on the pillow, her lips began to move back and forth as if she were moistening them and eyes, even the swollen eye, fluttered. Her tongue licked her lips and she sighed, before she finally opened her eyes.

She screamed when she saw Holliday and Shipman leaning over and staring down at her.

Wyatt suppressed a smile.

"Wh-who are you? Where am I?" she asked.

"We're with the Chicago Police Department Special Victims Unit. We're agents Shipman and Holliday,"

Shipman explained. "And you're at Chicago Medical Center. You were brought here because you were beaten in the lady's room at the Pied Piper Bar. Do you remember any of that? Nurse Patton would like permission to run a rape kit on you if you don't mind."

"A wh-wh-what?"

"To see if you were physically assaulted as well," Holliday added.

Oh geez, those two had the bed side manner that was sure to get them the results they wanted.

To his surprise Colleen consented and a curtain was drawn around her and the bed, blocking his view from where he sat. She didn't even know he was in the room yet. Which was for the best after her reaction to Shipman and Holliday. He'd introduce himself later.

He checked his phone, but kept his ears attuned to what was being said. Mainly Nurse Patton ensured that Colleen felt untraumatized by the exam as possible through the exam, made small talk, explaining what she was doing and how her skirt had been taken into evidence already and her panties and bra were needed as well. He'd see if Shipman and Holliday could pick Colleen up a pack of underwear and bring by here later. That couldn't be too much to ask of them.

When the curtain was pulled back, Colleen looked already fast asleep.

"Did you give her something to knock her out?" he asked.

"No. She passed out again. I'm sure she'll come

around soon. I'll get this sent to the lab. A doctor will be in shortly to see her."

Once the nurse left, Shipman touched him on the arm. "Don't look so concerned. The girl will be fine."

"How can you be so sure?"

"There was a look in her eye that told me she was made of strong stuff that something like this wasn't going to be the end of her."

Holliday snorted, shaking her head. "You and your looks."

"Don't mind her either. I know what I'm talking about," Shipman said.

Wyatt nodded and pulled out his wallet. He handed the woman a ten. "I heard the nurse tell Ms. Summers that she'd be taking her panties. I thought maybe you could pick her up a package and bring it back by here for me. I wouldn't know what to get."

"Sure thing. And that's a mighty fine gesture. The hospital will provide her a pair of sweat pants or scrubs to leave here in, but she'd be commando, if you know what I mean."

"Yeah. I do. Which wouldn't do much for her dignity at this point and all the more reason I think she needs the panties."

"Are you two finished with your hen party?" Holliday asked.

Shipman rolled her eyes. "Sure. I'm coming."

"We've got another case to get to. The captain just texted there's another rape case to investigate."

Shipman opened the door and Holliday went first.

They were a strange partnership, but it seemed to work for them. And as long as they got the job done making a case against the perpetrator that assaulted Ms. Summers, Wyatt didn't care how they did it.

He turned back toward the hospital bed where Colleen Summers lay. Her blonde hair was in disarray from the attack. He realized that while the curtain had been drawn the nurse had changed Colleen out of her blouse and put a hospital gown on her. He supposed they'd put all her outer clothes into evidence bags in the event trace evidence from the perp had been left on them.

She was a rather pretty girl from what he could tell minus the purple bruising covering one side of her face and the busted lip. He crossed his arms and paced the length of the room waiting for the doctor to come in, but when the door opened it was only Nurse Patton returning.

She halted in the doorway. "You're still here? I-I thought you were with Shipman and Holliday."

"No. I'm with the victim. I'm Wyatt Kincaid," he offered her his hand as she walked into the room. "I've been assigned to protect her by Commander Samuel Burns of the Chicago PD."

"Well. Well. This is a first. I've never known an assault victim to have a protector assigned by the PD. What gives? Is she someone famous?"

"No ma'am. But she was at the Pied Piper Bar where a gang shooting resulted in a murder."

"And attempted rape."

"Attempted. So that means she wasn't?"

"No. There was no sign of penetration. No fluids or tearing. She was lucky."

Wyatt let out a long breath and looked over at the bed where Colleen lay still sleeping. The nurse checked the machine writing down the vitals it displayed in her chart. She was finishing up when the doctor finally came in to check on Colleen and determined she needed to be admitted overnight to keep a check on her because of the trauma she'd suffered.

Before Colleen was admitted, a woman from registration stopped by.

"I'm sorry to bother you, but I understand Ms. Summers is unconscious and we need to determine if she has been a patient here before. I looked up her name in our patient records and we have a few Colleen Summers so I need to narrow it down."

"Her purse was stolen. She doesn't have any identification on her," he explained.

"I have been informed of that as well." The woman smiled and showed him a small device she held in her hand. "As it happens all I need to do is scan her fingerprint to see if she has registered here before. We started requiring all our patients to do this to link their records in the event they arrived without identification."

The woman walked over to the bed, sat her laptop on the rolling bedside tray, and began to scan Colleen's finger.

"Wait. Will it also give you her parents' information?" Wyatt asked.

"It does because she is in the system. Assuming she is the same Colleen Summers, she had an outpatient procedure with us last year."

"Would it be against hospital policy for me to have her parents' info so I can contact them and let them know she is here? And if it is, would you be able to contact them for that purpose?"

The woman nodded. "I can contact them, letting them know she has been admitted. Do you want them here now? Or will in the morning be sufficient? My shift ends at seven tomorrow morning. I can make myself a note to call before I get off."

"In the morning. There is no need for them to come now and be up all night when they can sleep. Someone should get some sleep."

The woman smiled again. "The patient room's arm chair pulls out into a sleeper so you can rest if you are staying the night."

"Thanks."

"It shouldn't be long now before they transfer her to a room."

Wyatt nodded, sat down in the folding chair in the ER room and waited for the transfer to happen once the woman left. She'd been nice. In fact, everyone he'd encountered, except for Holliday, had been friendly. It reminded him so much of the US military hospital where he'd stayed in Germany before being flown back to the states to rehab at Walter Reed.

His family had been notified by a stranger that he was there and he'd eventually received a phone call from his parents once he was conscious and verbal enough to make conversation without breaking down. Images of the Humvee explosion flashed through his head. The sand in the air. The screams and the heat of the moment as the sun beat down on him lying in the desert when the other Humvee pulled up, finding him half-conscious. His breathing was labored and he broke out in a cold sweat. His right leg bounced repeatedly in a nervous habit. He laid a hand on it to still it. He took in a slow, deep breath.

Damn.

This didn't need to be about his time after the IED explosion. He was here for Colleen. He was here to protect her, to help her deal with her trauma, not to relive his own ordeal.

He shook his head, dispelling the lingering images of him in a hospital bed, hooked up to the monitors, followed by the group therapy sessions. Leaning back in the chair, he rested his head against the wall and he closed his eyes, taking in a deep breath before letting it out slowly. He repeated this until all bad thoughts subsided and he felt more relaxed and in control.

· · ·

WYATT STARED BLANKLY at a sleeping Colleen trying to figure out what he was going to do if she didn't wake up from this semi-coma state anytime soon. The doctor last night seemed to think this was a trauma state. It allowed her mind to relax and heal from the ordeal so that when she did wake she could handle it better. Yet when the doctor came in this morning and found she had not come around he was concerned that this could mean she'd hit her head during the assault and there could be serious injury they were not aware of so testing was being ordered.

All of this waiting was doing little good for him and made him miss his service dog Ruby. Being away from Ruby for a week was the longest they'd been separated since he got her but bringing her on this trip had not been an option. His boss, Hank Patterson, had offered to watch Ruby while he was away. He just hoped that Hank's little girl Emma didn't turn Ruby into a softy by dressing her up like one of her dolls with a big bow around her neck. Heaven forbid Emma would insist Sadie paint Ruby's nails like her own a sparkling pink. The little girl loved playing with Ruby and his feisty dog loved the attention from the blonde headed child.

His phone buzzed and he pulled it out of his pocket to see who was trying to reach him. The text was from Brand wanting an update.

"Still at hospital. Colleen lost consciousness in ambulance, hasn't woken yet. EMT thought it was shock. Doctors are concerned it's more."

"Oh man. Keep us posted."

The door to the room slid open and Commander Burns escorted an older man and woman inside. The couple rushed over to the bed where Colleen lay and the woman started weeping.

Burns looked in Wyatt's direction before he left the room without saying a word.

Wyatt slowly got to his feet and walked over to introduce himself. "Are you Mr. and Mrs. Summers?"

"We are," the man said. "I'm Bob and this is Joan. And you are?"

"I'm Wyatt Kincaid. I've been assigned to protect your daughter. If you have a moment I'd like to discuss that with you."

"Protect her?" the woman said, her tears stopping. She wiped at her eyes with the Kleenex gripped in her right hand. "Why does she need protecting? The Commander never said anything about that when he came by the house."

"Maybe we should step out in the hall and find somewhere more private to talk so not to disturb her. We aren't sure what she can hear while unconscious and we wouldn't want to add to her discomfort."

"But we just got here," the woman complained. "No. You can explain yourself right here to us if it's concerning Colleen. I'm not leaving her side."

"Even if it's for the best?" Wyatt asked.

Mrs. Summer's mouth fell open as if she were about to say something but she didn't. "If the doctor believes she is better off having total silence and rest then I will leave."

"We'd never do anything to bring harm to our daughter," Mr. Summers said.

"I think I'll let you visit with her for a few minutes and then we can talk. I'd feel more comfortable discussing this in private."

Wyatt left them alone and went to the nurse's station across from the room. He recognized the nurse behind the counter as the one that had been assigned to Colleen that morning.

"Hey, Katy. I need to talk to Mr. and Mrs. Summers about their daughter. Is there a place where we can talk in private?"

"There's a room down near the elevators that is used for activities sometimes. It has a door you can close. Let me check the schedule and see if it's free." She typed something into the computer and looked back up at him. "It's free and I've put you in there for half-an-hour starting at half past the hour. Will that be enough time?"

"Yes. That should be plenty. Thanks." He walked back to Colleen's room giving her parents the extra time with her before asking them to follow him down the hallway to the private room.

He closed the door behind him and they sat in the chairs. "Like I said before, I'm Wyatt Kincaid. I'm a former SEAL who has been asked to watch over your daughter by Commander Burns. I'm part of the Brotherhood Protectors that have been asked to partner with the Chicago PD on a case. I'm not sure what he has told you about what happened to your daughter so I don't want to repeat any information you already know."

"He didn't tell us anything other than she was admitted last night after being beaten and her purse was stolen. That was the reason it took so long to contact us."

"Anyway, to make a long story short, Colleen was out with her friends last night at a bar. They were getting ready to leave when she went to the lady's room. Your daughter was assaulted by someone while in the lady's. We do not know who. While she was in there the bar was robbed by a gang, the bartender murdered."

"Oh, my baby," Mrs. Summers gasped.

"Was she—" Mr. Summers' question trailed off.

"No. The exam in the ER showed that she wasn't sexually assaulted. Her purse was stolen as well as her cell phone. She sustained scrapes and bruises and a busted lip. The main concern the doctor has right now is why she has not woken up. Why she continues to sleep. The ER nurse gave her a shot to wake her last night to get her consent to do the exam and while she performed it then Colleen slipped under again. The doctor feels like this is her way of dealing with the trauma."

"This is terrible. She should move back home with me," Mrs. Summers stated.

"Joan, don't go smothering her." Mr. Summers crossed his arms over his chest, looking annoyed at his ex-wife.

"I'm not. I think I should know what is best for my daughter. She needs love and support at a time like this. Living with me for a few months should give her that."

"And what if she decides she'd rather live with her father?" Mr. Summers asked. "She has a perfectly good right to want to do that, you know."

"Fine, Bob, if Colleen would rather live with you. I won't stand in her way. Does that make you happy?"

The two bickered back and forth about who should take Colleen home with them for a good five minutes or so until Wyatt gave a shrill whistle and shut them up.

"I think all of this arguing is pre-mature. Colleen needs to wake up. Snap out of whatever is keeping her asleep. Whether that means she needs therapy with a specialist who deals in rape and assault counseling, or she needs rest then we need to give that to her."

"She needs her mother that's what she needs and comfort food. Sleeping in her room at home surrounded by good memories," Mrs. Summers said.

"Oh sure. The house where we argued all the time," Mr. Summers got up and started pacing the floor. "That's just what Colleen needs. Being back under your thumb twenty-four hours a day, seven days a week. I think this young man knows more of what our daughter needs."

"How can you say that, Bob? He doesn't know us. He doesn't know Colleen. How can he possibly know what she needs?" Mrs. Summers asked, getting up and stalking up to him. She pointed a finger and jabbed it square in his chest. "It's just like you to side with anyone but me. That was always your problem when we were married. You wanted to be anywhere but with me."

Wyatt swallowed, afraid he was about to witness World War III commence and it was all his fault for bringing the two of them into this room.

"Listen, we don't have to make any decisions on where Colleen is going right now. I just wanted to explain to you why I was here. How Colleen ended up here and to let you know that her other friends Carly, Simone, and Jules made it out of the bar alive in the event you are interested. From what I understand, all three have been assigned a protector, my buddies, because they are potential witnesses in the bar shooting."

He watched as Mr. and Mrs. Summers looked at one another and then quickly and turned toward him, forgetting their argument as if it never even happened. It was the strangest thing he'd ever seen.

"Those poor girls. Are they okay?" Mrs. Summers asked. "We really are fond of each one of them. They have been so good for our Colleen."

"As far as I know they are. I saw all three of them last night and they looked to be perfectly fine. Shall we go back to check on Colleen now?"

The two nodded.

As they walked back down the corridor Mrs. Summers said. "I should reach out to Gloria and Patience to make sure Simone and Carly are doing okay. Maybe set up a lunch date for the three of us soon. It has been too long. Bob, it wouldn't hurt for you to try and contact Clayton Reid or even Leland, Simone's step-father. Heaven knows if you can pin-point Henry Manning down. He's always so busy at his law firm. We've really been out of touch with them all since the girls graduated college. Don't you remember how we'd go to dinner?"

"I don't think it really was the girls graduating college that put a stop to it, but Carly getting married. Don't you remember she married that douche bag from that country club?"

Mrs. Summers snickered. "Oh, Bob! You shouldn't say that, someone who knows that Justin Porter might overhear you."

Wyatt hung back letting them go into Colleen's room while he checked his phone and the text message that just came through. It was from Brand again. He was wanting an update on Colleen. He wasn't sure what he was going to tell him.

"Hey Wyatt," Katy said at the nurses' station.

He looked up from his phone and grinned.

35

"She's awake. The doctor is with her now. I thought you'd want to know."

"That's good. That's really good. Thanks for telling me."

Feeling hopeful, he began typing his message.

"She's awake. Doc with her now. Commander Burns located her parents. Bad mistake. Arguing over which one should take her home. Haven't told them she's not going with them."

"Take charge of the situation."

"Will do."

"Report back when you know more on Colleen's condition."

"Over and out."

He walked over to the counter and smiled down at Katy again. "Is that room available again later?"

"All day. Do you think you'll need it again?" Katy asked.

He nodded. "It's a good possibility."

"Just let me or one of the other nurses know and we'll put you in there."

"Thanks."

MR. AND MRS. SUMMERS weren't thrilled when Wyatt asked them to go back down the hall to the activities room to talk again, but now that he knew what the doctor's plan of action was for Colleen he wanted to let her parents know they weren't taking her home.

They had not even gotten into the room when Mrs. Summers turned on Mr. Summers and started her attack on how she should be the one to take Colleen home with her. Mr. Summers threw his hands up in the air and walked across the room shaking his head as he repeated over and over.

"I'm not listening to this. I'm not listening to this."

Wyatt had never seen two middle-aged adults act more childish than these two people. It was like they had not already gone through this an hour before and were going through it again for the first time. He felt so sorry for Colleen and he was more determined than ever that she should not go home with either one of these looney toons.

He gave a sharp pitched whistle, cutting them off. "Enough," he said. "I know you want what's best for your daughter, but this isn't it." He shut the door to the room rather loudly and planted his hands on his hips. "Colleen is not going home with either one of you. I'm taking her to Montana to a safe house. I'll keep you informed of her progress in recuperating, but I believe this is for the best."

"Montana!" Mr. and Mrs. Summers said in unison before looking at one another in disbelief.

"You heard me right. Montana. She'll get clean, fresh mountain air there, peace and quiet open space and therapy to recovery from the trauma she's suffered. Plus, she won't have to worry that her attacker will find her apartment and come looking for her again. Don't argue with me. My mind is made up. If you do, I'll talk to Commander Burns about taking out an order of protection against you to keep you away from her until she has recovered. Your constant arguing will do more harm than good for her."

"You can't do that," Mr. Summers said.

"Wanna bet?"

"Can we see her again before she goes?" Mrs. Summer asked.

"Yes. I suggest you come alone."

They looked at one another and then nodded in agreement.

Wyatt walked them to the elevator and then headed back to Colleen's room. He was looking forward to a little peace and quiet himself after his encounter with the Summers. He'd slid the door to her room only a fraction when he heard a warm, female voice that stopped him.

"Honey, we don't know. Do you remember going out with us on Friday night?"

"Yes. I remember dancing with you guys, but that's it," a second, softer voice said.

"We were getting ready to leave, but you had to go to the restroom," a third sultry voice said. "So, you went alone."

"We waited for you out front at the bar, but then the bar got robbed. The bartender was shot and we were lucky to have gotten out alive," the warm first voice said. "In all the chaos, we never knew what happened to you. We found out you were taken to the hospital last night to be checked out."

"Your parents are here, down the hall arguing about who is going to take you home. Have you seen them yet?" the third voice asked.

There was a groan. "Carly, I know I made fun of your apartment last night but let me go home with you."

They laughed.

Wyatt smiled at their closeness.

"Hey, you're remembering something from last night. That's good," the first voice said. "What did the doctor say when he saw you this morning?"

"That I needed to rest and stay here another day because of my memory loss and some tests they want to run on me."

Wyatt established from the conversation that the second voice was Colleen, he liked the sound of it.

"Did they examine you?" the third voice asked.

There was a slight pause before Colleen responded. Wyatt leaned his head against the glass door frame, waiting to see how she handled the question.

"I wasn't... That didn't happen. I still feel violated. I don't remember it, but it feels like something horrible happened. I want to shower a dozen times. I know I never want to wear that skirt again."

He let out the breath he hadn't realized he was holding. *Good girl, express your feelings. Get it off your chest. Don't hold it in.*

He decided this was the time to make his presence known. He pushed the sliding door open further, yanked the curtain back fast as he stepped fully into the room catching all three of them off guard.

"Ladies, I don't assume you were given permission to be here?"

"Are you going to do something about it?" The feisty redhead walked toward him, stopping when she was nose to nose with him.

Wyatt ignored her, sliding the glass room door shut before he pulled out his phone and punched in a number. Then he put the phone up to his ear. "Don Juan, I think you've lost something very important. You need to come to collect it now before I report you to Brand for slacking on your duties. It has red hair and …"

He laughed at Don Juan's reaction. "See you then."

"Who's he?" Colleen asked from across the room.

"He's your protector," Carly explained. "We've all got a guy assigned to protect us after what happened last night at the bar."

"Really? Why?"

"The bar shooting was gang-related. Simone and I are witnesses. Jules saw the getaway car outside because she came back when she heard the gunshot."

"I heard it too."

"You did?"

Colleen nodded, closing her eyes. "That's what caused my attacker to run away."

Wyatt came over to the bed. "Did she say what I think she said?"

Carly nodded.

"Colleen, I'm Wyatt Kincaid your protector, what else do remember from last night?" he asked.

"I'm tired. I need to rest now." She pulled the sheet up and scooted under the cover more.

Wyatt punched in a few more numbers on his phone and walked back toward the sliding doors. "Brand, Wyatt here. You need to come to Chicago Med. There's been a development. Sure. Get here as fast as you can. Thanks."

He turned around and looked at them. "Ladies, you might as well take a seat and get comfortable. You're gonna be here a while. And then you won't be able to sit without remembering the chewing out you get."

WYATT KEPT a lookout on the clock while half-watching Carly and Simone whisper to one another as Colleen napped waiting for Brand and Don Juan to arrive. The time clicked by slowly that Colleen woke again and the three started talking again. He'd even been able to ask her a few more questions about last night. He couldn't understand what was taking Brand and Don Juan so long to get to the hospital. Finally, he thought he heard their voices out in the corridor, so he walked to the sliding glass door and pushed it aside, going out of the room before closing the door back.

"I thought I heard voices." Wyatt was surprised to see they weren't alone. That Commander Burns was with them. "Before you go in there chewing the girls out for leaving you, their visit has been good for Colleen. She's been responsive. She has even remembered things about last night with them that my questioning couldn't get her to recall. I know they disobeyed and risked their lives coming here. I still would bring the wrath of God down on them, but keep in mind what good was accomplished."

"Did she get a good look at her attacker? Should we bring down a sketch artist?" Hawkeye asked.

"She hasn't mentioned that yet, but she did say she heard the gunshot and that is why her attacker ran off. She has napped. When she woke she talked of her attacker taking her purse. She's afraid of her credit cards getting maxed out. She's also concerned about her apartment and getting robbed. That's the reason I contacted your office, Commander."

"I was in the area so I dropped by to see how things were going."

"How did her parents take the news she wasn't going home with them?" Brand asked.

"Not well. When I explained she wasn't going to her apartment, but a safe house, they agreed. In return, I promised to keep them well aware of what was going on with her." *With a little persuading.*

"You handled that well, Kincaid." Hawkeye stepped forward and touched him on the shoulder. "Let's go in and meet this courageous young woman and her daring friends under better circumstances."

Wyatt pushed the curtain aside allowing Brand, Don Juan and Hawkeye to enter Colleen's room before him. Carly and Simone sat in straight back chairs across the room. Colleen turned her head toward the doorway when they entered.

"This is Commander Burns from Chicago PD, Brand Chambers, and Liam Donovan," Wyatt explained. "They are here to collect Simone and Carly."

"What if we don't want to go?" Simone asked.

"You'll do what you're told, young woman or I'll have you taken down to central booking," Hawkeye told her.

"On what charges?" she challenged.

"Impeding an investigation."

"And how would I be doing that?"

"By causing more work for your protector and the police to make sure you're safe. My officers need to be out in the field looking for your friend's attacker, not to mention the gang members who tried to rob the Pied Piper. I'm sure I could come up with other charges to keep you in a holding cell until we find the perps if it means keeping you safe. Or you can go back to your apartment with Mr. Donovan and stay in comfort. Is that reason enough for you to see you should be in your apartment where it is safe?" Commander Burns explained.

"I do have to go back to work Monday."

"Then he'll go with you." Commander Burns said. "I'll send a driver and a car around."

"I have a job interview next week. I need this job to pay my bills. Please, can I keep the interview?" Carly asked.

"No. Not after this stunt," Brand barked.

"Brand, take it down a notch." Commander Burns arched a brow at him, before turning toward Carly. "I don't see why that should be a problem if Brand goes with you. We want you to carry on your normal routine as much as possible. The two of you aren't under house arrest by any means. But we do want to keep you both safe and we're trying to take measures to ensure that. If it feels like your wings of freedom are clipped short-term, that's all it is—a temporary situation. Can you both understand that? Coming here today was a risk neither of you should have taken."

"Thank you, Commander." Carly swallowed. "There is one more thing. I'd like to be able to go to the bartender's funeral whenever that is to pay my respects to his wife if possible. Can that be arranged?"

The Commander was hesitant for a moment, but he finally nodded. "That can happen, Ms. Manning. I'm sure his wife will appreciate that."

CHAPTER 4

COLLEEN WATCHED and listened to what was going on in the room feeling like a spectator, finding it hard to keep up with her head feeling all muddled. And then the commander was talking to her, asking her questions. Her heart began to race and she found it difficult to breathe as the thump, thump, thumping of her blood beat in her ears.

Thankfully, Carly came over and took her hand, and the thunderous thumping subsided enough that she was able to hear what the commander was asking. Something about her attacker. A sickening feeling threatened to make her lose whatever contents was in her stomach and she steeled herself to focus on something other than the dark vision of the man bursting in on her in the ladies' room.

"I-I'm not sure what he looked like. He came through the door so fast and hit me in the face with his hand. I-I don't think I'd be any help for a sketch artist." Her words came tumbling out and she wasn't sure if she made any sense at all.

"You may think that now, but I'd like you to try. We can bring in a behavioral scientist who can take you on a journey through a series of questions. The results will help you reveal more than you ever imagined you'd remember."

"Like a profiler?" Colleen asked. "Something like they do on *Criminal Minds*?"

The commander nodded. "But this method is real."

"How soon can you have someone here?" the one Carly called her protector asked. What had Carly said his name was? Colleen tried to remember but concentrating made her head hurt.

"I can arrange to get someone here as early as this afternoon. The sooner we can get a sketch of her attacker, the better we'll be able to find him."

"When do you think Colleen will be released from the hospital?" Carly ventured to ask.

"That is up to the doctor," her protector said. "He wasn't hopeful this morning but that was because he wanted to run tests."

"So, her staying here has nothing to do with trying to keep her in a safe location?" Carly questioned.

"If that was what we were going for, we'd have to have a guard posted outside her door to track who comes in and out of this room. A hospital is too public to be safe." The commander turned to the one called

Brand. "My car and driver are downstairs. You and Donovan can escort the women to their respective apartments for now. I'll order a car detail for you both to have at your disposal. All you have to do is call when you want it. I'll send both of you the information."

"Thanks, Hawkeye." Brand motioned to Carly. "Say your good-byes so we can head out."

She nodded and looked down at Colleen, giving her hand a squeeze. "I'll see you soon. I know you're in good hands with Wyatt. You can call me if you want to talk."

Wyatt. That was his name. Why had it been so hard to recall?

"Good luck on your interview," Colleen said, squeezing Carly's hand back.

"Thanks. I'll need it." Carly stepped away from the bed and turned toward Simone. "Let's go girl."

"You're going to let him order you around like that?" Simone questioned.

"He's not ordering me around. It's time to go. Colleen needs to rest. Can't you see how tired she looks?"

"Simone!" the one the commander had called Donovan said, his tone full of irritation.

Colleen saw Simone's head snap in his direction.

"Yes, Donnie?" Simone purred.

Brand repeated. "Donnie?"

Again, Colleen felt like she was watching a side show as her friends got ready to leave. So much was going on around her that she didn't fully understand. Too many looks. Too much innuendo. She was glad she had gotten to see Carly and Simone and that they were okay. She hoped Jules was too.

She fell asleep again soon after they left but found herself in a fitful sleep as images from her past haunted her. It all started with her shamefully walking home sometime in the wee hours of the morning from the fraternity house barefoot, carrying her strappy heels, her dress torn at the shoulder. The disbelief of what had happened to her flooded through her as she cried and stumbled her way toward the sorority house. One moment she was outside, the next she was in her bathroom staring at her mascara smeared face. She couldn't remember how she made it into the sorority house or how she'd gotten to her room without anyone seeing the condition she was in. She'd undressed and thrown her dress and under garments in the trash before taking a hot, hot shower.

When the water hit her face, the man who barged in the lady's room slapped her across the face and forced himself on her. One second it was him, the next she was being pushed onto the floor in the basement of the fraternity house. Two eyes stared at her, bored deep into her soul. She shook her head, closed her eyes, and tried to get away from those eyes, but when she looked again, they were still there hovering over her.

She gasped, coming wide awake. Her heart raced. Looking around she saw she was alone in the room and she wondered where Wyatt, her protector was at the moment. She didn't want to be alone right now. It would have been nice to have had him near.

BY THE TIME her dinner tray was delivered she was exhausted. Orderly after orderly had arrived all afternoon to take her for the tests that the doctor had ordered. Then she'd had to work with the sketch artist trying to give a description of her attacker, even though she didn't get a good look at him. She'd told the commander that, but he'd assured her the sketch artist would be able to ask her questions to produce a full sketch. The end result had been those two eyes and a nose that she knew didn't belong to her attacker but the frat boy that had raped her in college. She'd had nightmares about those eyes for almost a year after the attack and had thought she'd pushed them far back into the recesses of her mind. Until now. Until this.

"You're not eating. Would you like something different?" Wyatt asked. "I'm going to run down to the cafeteria and get something before it closes. I could bring you something back."

She glanced his way and tried to smile. He'd been very attentive all day and tried to make her feel at ease. It had been nice not to be all alone.

"I'm fine. I'm sure the food is fine. I'm just tired. Not much of an appetite really."

He got to his feet and came over to her bed. "I don't

want to sound like a broken record, but you need to eat something. You didn't touch your lunch tray. That burger looked good and you let that lime Jell-O go to waste. That looks like pretty good beef stew there. I'm sure it isn't as good as Cookie's back on the ranch, but you should at least take a few bites."

"Cookie?"

"Carl Fite, he's the ranch cook at the Brighter Days Rehabilitation Ranch in Eagle Rock, Montana. It's down the road from where I work. The guys and I sometimes go over there and help out and we eat, especially when they have a barbeque."

"What kind of rehabilitation do they do at the ranch?"

"They take in beaten and abused horses and nurture them back to health. The ranch is facilitated with disabled veterans. Some have physical limitations due to injury from being in theater and others have the unseen kind that can be more harmful. They may be there on a temporary basis until they learn to cope and get back on their feet or it may be a long-term stay. In the end the healing that goes on at the ranch benefits them all. The horses get the loving care they need and the care-givers despite their limitations feel useful because maybe they couldn't hold down a full-time job."

"That sounds wonderful."

Wyatt nodded. "The ranch also helps trauma victims. I'd like to take you there when you are discharged to get you away from the city. Just think about it. You can give me your answer in a day or two. Now I'm going to go get some grub."

Colleen's heart raced at the thought of leaving Chicago and going to Montana, but it slowly subsided as she watched him leave the room. He'd approached the subject so easily with her, talking about the beef stew on her tray. He was sly. She'd have to watch him.

She looked down at the bowl and picked up the fork, stabbing a chunk of potato before putting it in her mouth and chewing. The seasoning wasn't bad. It needed more salt and pepper. She opened up the wrapped condiments pack on the tray and added a little of both to the bowl before taking another chunk of potato. Much better.

She thought about the horses at the ranch. She'd never been around a horse before and wasn't sure if she could provide the care they needed, but she'd learn if she went with him to Montana. The thought of riding a horse also intimidated her. Again, she'd learn while there. If she went. He'd said it was ultimately her decision. She had the option not to go. At least he wasn't forcing her. She liked that.

She had her two jobs to think about. The one she had and the one she was applying for. Her second interview was coming up later in the week. She was certain they'd want it to be an in-person meeting and not long-distance. That alone was enough reason for her to stay in Chicago. But her attacker had her purse. Her keys to her apartment.

When she finished with the tray she pushed the stand away and leaned her head back on the pillow, closing her eyes for a few moments before Wyatt returned. Leaving Chicago for a while wouldn't be bad. She rarely went on vacation. It would do her good to travel. See another state. Experience a new surrounding for a few weeks. It would give her some time to get over what had happened Friday night. Forget the dark image in her mind that dared to creep in whenever she let her guard down. Erase those eyes that were still lurking in her subconscious.

She balled her fists by her side.

Damn. She couldn't believe those eyes had shown up in that drawing. The ones from the frat house so long ago.

What if he was her attacker? What if he had been at the Pied Piper and had recognized her somehow and followed her to the lady's room, busting in on her and decided he had to have her one more time?

The thought made her shake and her lips began to tremble, she clenched at the bedsheets, twisting them in her grasp. No, please God. Don't let her attacker be him. Don't let him have found her after all these years. She'd been so careful, keeping her phone number listed as only C. Summers in the directory. She'd never told a soul, just like he'd warned her not to. It had been her secret, her burden to carry.

She wept, turning over on her left side, hiding her face in the pillow.

SHE MUST HAVE DOZED off because the next thing she knew she heard soft talking in her room. She used the edge of the sheet to wipe away any remaining tears before she turned to see who was in her room. It was Wyatt talking to a woman she vaguely remembered from Friday night. But everything was so hazy from when she was first brought into the hospital.

"Colleen, good to see you again," the woman said, coming to her bedside. "I'm SV Detective Shipman. I don't suppose you remember me from the ER? I dropped by to bring something for you and to see how you are doing."

"Thank you."

"Holliday, didn't want to come with you?" Wyatt asked, holding a brown paper bag.

Colleen assumed the bag must have been whatever Shipman had brought for her.

"She's finishing up some paperwork on the case we were called to last night."

"A good enough excuse not to see me again," Wyatt said.

Colleen found that funny, but she couldn't laugh, she didn't have the energy. Shipman had no trouble laughing.

"Holliday has men issues for a reason. Our line of

work and her past, but that's all I'm saying on that," Shipman said.

"Maybe she needs counseling."

"She's gone. Personal and on the job mandated. But nothing is going to work until she's ready to let it work."

"True," Wyatt agreed. "Thanks again for getting these for Colleen."

Colleen took the bag from him and slowly looked inside. It was a package of three pairs of panties. She hadn't realized she wasn't wearing any and she felt her cheeks warm.

"Thank you both," she murmured.

"It was my pleasure, honey. Thank Wyatt for thinking of it. I better get going. Good luck to you," Shipman said and then left them.

Colleen stared at the package in the brown bag and started to cry again. She felt silly, but it was the nicest gesture anyone could have made.

CHAPTER 5

WYATT HEARD COLLEEN crying and turned in her direction trying to figure out what had brought this on, but saw she was clutching the paper bag to her. "Hey now, no need to cry over it. Hopefully Shipman knew the right size. That's why I asked her to get them."

Colleen shook her head back and forth, put the back of one hand up to her mouth and sniffed a few times, squeezing her eyes shut tight. Letting her hand drop, she gasped for breath. "I-I-I know. But yo-you-you're so kind to think of me in this way."

"I was thinking of your dignity." He sat at the foot of the bed and laid a warm hand on her feet.

She nodded, laying her head back against the pillow still clutching the paper bag. "Tell me more about Montana. Did you grow up there?"

"No. I'm from Virginia. I'm surprised you couldn't

hear it in my voice. I picked up a thick accent during my four years at The Citadel."

"Impressive. Tell me again what your connection is with the Chicago PD?"

"I just told you I was sent by them to watch over you. I'm not a police officer. Ex-military medically discharged."

"But you have ties in Montana?"

"That's right. The Brotherhood Protectors are a group of men and women who have been medically discharged but still want to serve their country doing what they love to do, but because of their injuries may not be able hold down a normal job. Hank Patterson, my boss, he created the Brotherhood Protectors and brought all these amazing men and women from different branches of service together in Eagle Rock. He looks for the best of the best, the most elite skill sets that our country can't afford to lose because of a physical injury. We provide security, protection and more as needed depending on the job.

You met Brand and Liam earlier today. They are assigned to protect Carly and Simone. Will is with your friend Jules. We're all part of the team that came out to do a demonstration for the Chicago PD to show how the Brotherhood Protectors could be useful to a metro city. Commander Burns was a former SEAL in the day. He went through training with Brand. So, we had an in there and when Burns got the call about the Pied Piper shooting, he tapped us to put our skills to use because he'd like to start a program in his district."

"So, he's using us as guinea pigs."

Wyatt grinned. "Are you trying to be funny, Ms. Summers?"

"Can't slip nothing past you." She half-smiled. "So, if Brand is a former SEAL, what are you and your other teammates?"

"I was in the SEALs as well. Liam's from the Marines and Will is a retired Army Ranger."

She yawned. "I'm sorry. I'm very tired. It has been a long day. I really do want to hear more about your Brotherhood Protectors and Montana. Maybe tomorrow?"

"Sure. You get some rest. We've got plenty of time to talk."

He stood, pulled the knit blanket up to her waist, and then dimmed the light over the headboard so it wasn't shining in her eyes.

He made himself comfortable in the armchair where he'd slept and waited until he was certain Colleen was asleep before he called the Brighter Days Ranch hoping to catch Hannah in her office. She liked to take time on Saturday afternoons to finish up on her client notes from the weekly physical therapy sessions she held. So, there was a good chance he'd get her on the phone, unless Davila had whisked her away for a romantic weekend for two.

The line rang three or four times, but he was

patient. He knew that sometimes it could only ring once or twice on the other end.

"Brighter Days Rehabilitation Ranch, Hannah speaking, how can I help you?"

"Hannah, this is Wyatt Kincaid. I hope I haven't caught you at a bad time."

"No, Wyatt. Not at all. Did Hank reach you already?"

"Hank? No. He hasn't. Did something happen to Ruby?" He jumped up from his seat and started pacing the floor.

"No. No. Ruby is fine. Hank and Emma were by here this afternoon with her and she's doing good, missing you of course, but otherwise fine. I was asking about you coming to work at the ranch for a few weeks. I have a new resident that will need your assistance settling in."

"Thank God. I've been nervous about leaving Ruby." Wyatt knew he was rambling so he stopped pacing and forced himself to sit down. "Funny you should be wanting that. I'll make you a deal. I'll come work for you if you'll take a civilian client while I'm there. I know it isn't policy, but I've been assigned to protect her and she's been assaulted, beaten, not raped. Yet, there is something going on with her. I can tell. She needs to get away from here and her bickering parents."

"Okay, Wyatt. You had me at you'd been assigned to protect her and the fact you were calling me. I'll make room for her. In the main house so she will feel safe. You and Ruby can have one of the cabins. If anyone understands what the Brotherhood Protectors do it's me."

"Thanks, Hannah."

"When should I expect you?"

"As soon as they release Colleen from the hospital. I'm hoping we'll be there by Wednesday at the latest."

"See you then," Hannah said before the line went dead.

Wyatt put his phone down and looked over at a sleeping Colleen. "I've done my part. Now it's all up to you to get well enough for the doctor to release you."

WYATT WOKE the next morning to the sound of female giggles. He first thought he was dreaming that Carly and Simone were still there with Colleen, but as he became more coherent, he realized there really was someone in the room with her and the two were giggling. Opening his eyes, he listened intently trying to pinpoint if he recognized the voice. He did. He'd heard it before. In fact, he was certain he'd heard it yesterday.

He pushed himself up to a sitting position and dared to look over at Colleen's bed. Sure enough her mother was in the room with them. But at least she'd listened and come alone. He did not see Mr. Summers hanging around.

"I hope we didn't wake you?" Mrs. Summers called, leaning her head close to Colleen's.

"No. It's time I got up." He stood and headed to the bathroom to splash cold water on his face, but then recalled after he closed the door there wasn't a sink in the facility, it was out in the room with Colleen and her mother. He chalked his forgetfulness up to inconvenient hospital rooms and lack of sleep. The pullout in the chair wasn't the best place to crash, but he had slept on worse.

When he opened the door and walked to the sink he noticed Colleen was alone. "Your mother didn't have to leave because I was awake."

"She was on her way to church. She goes to the early service, my father to the later that way they don't have to run into each other or change churches."

Wyatt nodded, turned on the water and washed his hands. He splashed water on his face, reached for a few of the paper towels in the dispenser and blotted his face dry, before turning back to speak to her. "They argue too much."

"I know, but they can't seem to help it. It's a miracle we make it through weekly brunch together."

"Your mom needs to find closure."

Colleen nodded. "Exactly. I've felt that way for years. I even told her to seek counseling, but she just laughs it off. She's convinced her problems left when my father moved out."

"Clearly that didn't happen or she wouldn't keep

harping on him every time she sees him." Wyatt crossed his arms over his chest.

Colleen giggled. "I like you. Mom said you had her number and I believe she was right. However, she is trying to convince me I need to come stay with her instead of going to Montana with you."

"She didn't..."

"Don't worry. I told her I'd already made up my mind to go. Which I have. The thought of going back to my apartment right now is not something I want. Neither is staying with either of my parents."

"Good to hear because I've got us all squared away in Montana. Your spot at the Brighter Days Ranch is secured and I've been hired on to work as a counselor there. You'll be in the main house while Ruby and I will be in one of the cabins on the property."

"Great. I can't wait."

He tossed the used paper towel in the trash. "I'm going to go find coffee. Preferably something besides what the hospital gives us. Would you like a cup?"

"Yes please."

"I'll be back. Don't run off now." He grinned and gave her a wink.

She smiled and looked to her left.

Maybe he shouldn't have winked, but he was trying to lighten the mood after discussing her parents arguing. He felt they'd made a connection there. And it was good to hear Colleen tell him she'd already decided she'd rather go to Montana with him to the ranch than stay with her own bickering parents. For someone who had been through what she had that was a big step. But he suspected it was the draw of the ranch and not wanting to go back to her own place that was fueling her desire to get away. More than her thinking about having to travel with a total male stranger after what she'd just been through.

But then, Shipman said she'd looked into Colleen's eyes in the ER and saw that the woman was made of stronger stuff that something like this wasn't going to break her. And if anyone should know after working hundreds of SV cases it should be Shipman.

CHAPTER 6

COLLEEN WONDERED who this Ruby was waiting for Wyatt back in Montana. He hadn't mentioned her before today. He didn't wear a wedding ring but most men didn't these days. So, did that make Ruby his girlfriend? Not that she was interested. She wasn't. Not after what had happened to her. It had taken her two years to be able to date after the first time and she never got physical, nothing more than a good night kiss. So, she had plenty of first dates and a few relationships that lasted a couple of weeks, but the guy soon lost interest when she couldn't commit to anything more.

She couldn't imagine feeling comfortable with a man again except Wyatt of course. He was different. He was here to protect her. There was a clear boundary. An already established line of trust.

Yes, she could trust him to take her to the Brighter

Days Ranch where she could get the help she needed. Every time she allowed herself to think about what happened fatigue engulfed her and the only way to get over it was to sleep. She closed her eyes, and sleep came quickly, but didn't last long uninterrupted.

She thought she heard Wyatt talking to someone, but she had difficulty opening her eyes. Her eye lids felt weighted as if she were drugged. Had the nurse given her something in her IV this morning?

The voices sounded lyrical to her and soon was replaced by music, she was dancing with Simone at the Pied Piper on the stage doing the wave to Ed Sheeran one second and the next she was walking down the darkened hallway to the lady's room. Bright light filled her vision and she heard weeping, pleading as darkness settled all around her and all she saw was those eyes above her, looking down at her as his two friends held her down so he could drive into her as she screamed, "Stop. No, don't. Stop. Please stop."

"Colleen. Sh-h-h. It's okay."

Hands reached for her and she fought them away.

"Colleen, it's Wyatt. You're having a bad dream. Everything is going to be okay. Just open your eyes."

She heard her name, but everything else sounded like loud music blasting in her ears as she struggled against her attacker, music from the frat party upstairs. Why had she stupidly gone down in the basement to see their prized trophy case? So what if their acapella group won three straight years in the choral festival.

She had to get away from him and his friends. She had to get free. Why couldn't she get free? Why wouldn't he stop his ravaging of her? Why? Why?

WYATT CLIMBED onto the bed and pulled Colleen to him, holding her close in his arms trying to soothe her. When the nurse returned she brought the doctor with her.

"I hear she had an outburst. Good thing I was on my way here to see her," the doctor said looking at his tablet "Her chart shows she just had a sedative so we can't give her anything more right now. But it obviously brought back something to mind as she slept. I'll try to get a psych consult for her today or tomorrow. With it being Sunday it depends who's on call. It won't hurt for her to talk to someone while she's here."

"Whatever you think," Wyatt said, slipping back off the bed and tucking Colleen under the covers now that she had quietened.

After the doctor left, he settled in the armchair and drank his coffee thinking about her outburst and how she'd fought against him at first before she'd finally relaxed, allowing him to comfort her. The episode occurred while she slept which meant she probably wouldn't even remember it when she woke. And if the doctor was right and it had been brought on by the sedative she was given, then perhaps her dosage needed to be adjusted. He doubted a psych consult was even needed. He'd really only agreed because he thought it would be good for Colleen to talk to someone professionally before they got to the Brighter Days Ranch. It would get her primed to begin therapy out there. He'd request she work with Ellie Danner, an ex-Special Forces tiger when she needed to be, but a care giver through and through. The woman was just the type that Colleen needed.

He finished his coffee and reached for Colleen's since she still had not woken. There was no need to let it get too cold to drink. He leaned back in the chair, closed his eyes and let his mind wonder. It didn't take long until he found himself back in the desert of Afghanistan on that last mission. Roberts was driving, McCaffrey was riding shotgun, while Stark was in the back with him. It was a routine drive. Another Humvee with four more of their troop members was following not far behind. McCaffrey decided he wanted to listen to some music and turned the volume up as he and Stark sang along to the song. Wyatt was watching for markers along the way. A loud beep, beep came over their radios and Roberts shut off the music so they could hear the message from command, but nothing came.

All Wyatt remembered was a loud explosion like a bomb going off. Sand flying in the air. Him being ejected from the Humvee and sailing 25-50 feet away from it, but still being able to feel the heat from where it burned once he came around. Screams from Roberts and Stark vibrated inside his head, even though he was told they died instantly on impact of the explosion. He shouldn't be able to have heard them. Yet he swore he did. Still. McCaffrey. He was blown to smithereens. There was no trace of him left.

Wyatt tried to take another sip of coffee, his hand shook so much it was hard to contact his mouth until he steadied his wrist with his other hand. The question he knew he'd never get the answer to was why he was the one that survived the explosion? Why had he been thrown from the Humvee when the bomb went off? Why him? Why?

He sat the insulated cup down and got out of the chair, pacing the room as he calmed his breathing, but it didn't stop his questioning why he was alive and his other troop mates were dead. It was something he found he always questioned even when he felt maybe God knew he was going to become a Brotherhood Protector and do good for others with his life after he left the SEALs. Not that any of the others couldn't have done the same thing. Yet, this still did not keep him from questioning why.

He looked at Colleen who was still sleeping and knew he couldn't sit around here all day. Grabbing his tactical bag and duffel he went out to the nurses' station. "I don't suppose you could point me in the direction of the nearest diner and laundry mat?"

. . .

WHEN WYATT RETURNED LATER that afternoon, he stopped by the nurses station again to check in and found out that Colleen's dad had dropped by to see her, but she'd been asleep so he hadn't stayed long.

He sent a text to Brand letting him know how things were, then he gave a call to Commander Burns to see if anything had turned up from the sketch taken the day before.

"Hey, Wyatt. Good to hear from you," Burns said. "Nothing yet from the sketch, but we have been running it through facial recognition to see if there is a match in the system. We'll bring them in for questioning and do a lineup if we believe there is good enough reason."

"I hope you find someone before we leave for Montana."

"Montana? Wait, you didn't clear this with me."

That wasn't something he'd needed to do. He normally had full range when he was on assignment.

"Sorry. Hank lets us use our judgement in these cases and I feel Colleen is safest away from Chicago. She's afraid to go back to her apartment and her parents aren't an option." He took a deep breath before explaining the situation to Commander Burns.

"I see your point there and this ranch is ready to take her?" Burns questioned.

"Yes. I've already squared it away."

"But you will return?" Burns asked.

"Of course. I'll bring her back when she is ready."

"I want you part of my Chicago Protection Task Force. This is the test run, you understand that, Kincaid. The Pied Piper case came at an opportune time for me to utilize you guys and show Chicago what you told us about in the weeklong workshop."

"I understand, Commander Burns."

"Good. Get our girl well so she can come back home. I'll keep in touch."

The line went dead and Wyatt stared across the room where Colleen still lay sleeping. He'd been offered two different jobs this week. One at the ranch and now this one in Chicago. Doors were opening up for him everywhere just like Hank had promised they would when the time was right. He wondered if Burns had discussed his plans to steal the four of them away from Hank yet. That would be an interesting conversation.

CHAPTER 7

Colleen sat in a wheelchair Monday morning after her psych eval in the waiting room for the orderly to return her to her room. She was surprised when Wyatt showed up to push her back instead.

"How did it go?" he asked.

"How do you think it went? She asked me all kinds of questions like I could possibly explain why a sedative to help me relax caused me to have a bad dream or nightmare while I slept and made me lash out in my sleep."

"You sound very upset by it."

"Wouldn't you be upset if you were given a medication that resulted in you being required to have a psych consult? I'm not crazy. I was attacked. It is only natural to have bad dreams or nightmares afterward."

"No one thinks you're crazy, Colleen," he said, leaning down close to her ear as he pushed the wheelchair. "You were attacked and that leaves a person bruised, mentally and physically. It takes time to heal. Which your body is already doing. I don't know if you've taken a good look in the mirror or not, but the bruising is slowly going away around your eye. Your busted lip is no longer as swollen. As these physical bruises vanish so will the memory of the assault when you close your eyes. Talking about it will help. That is why counseling is good. This consult was good."

She supposed he was right, but she didn't like seeing those two eyes when she closed her own. They brought bad memories from her past with them.

"Remember. You can talk to me about anything that you feel comfortable. We'll have plenty of time here and in Montana."

"We will?"

"Sure. You, me, the horses. You, me, and Ruby."

Colleen nodded. *Yeah, you, me, and Ruby.* She wanted to know more about Ruby, but something made her not ask. Instead she told him something else.

"I see his eyes when I close mine."

Wyatt stopped pushing the wheelchair and came around to the front so he was looking at her. He squatted in front of her and reached for her hands. "That will fade in time too. I promise. You may feel sometimes like it never will, but it will happen."

"How can you sound so sure of that? You haven't been...." She stopped herself before she said more and looked away from him. His soft imploring eyes that made her feel safe were nothing more than part of his job. He'd been assigned to protect her. It was his job. Outside of that did he really care about her?

"I survived a Humvee explosion in Afghanistan. I was the only survivor. That haunts me still. I question why me? Why not one of the other three members of my team?"

She looked back at him swiftly; surprised by his confession. "I'm sorry. I had no idea. I shouldn't have said..."

"It's okay. You don't know my past. I don't know yours." He stood and walked back to begin pushing the wheelchair again. "Let's get back to your room. It's almost lunch time for you."

She nodded, feeling awful for what she'd said, but before she could beat herself up over it she heard him say.

"If we don't get out of here today I'm going to order a pizza for us and have it delivered tonight. How does that sound?

"A master plan."

"All right then."

AFTER LUNCH, Colleen took a nap, but woke a short time later to find Commander Burns was in her room talking to Wyatt.

"I hope we didn't wake you," Wyatt said when she raised her hospital bed to a sitting position.

"No. I didn't even hear you until I woke," she said. "Hello, Commander Burns. Any news for us today?"

"Actually, that is why I came by. We found your purse with all its contents tossed in a dumpster only a few blocks away from the Pied Piper Bar. From what we can tell, the only thing you have lost is your cellphone. It is here, but destroyed."

The commander handed her the purse and showed her the damaged cell phone which he had in a large clear evidence bag. "Would you mind looking through your purse and letting me know if everything is there, if not, we will file an incident report."

"Of course." Colleen opened her purse, noticing a patch of powder residue on the front. Had they taken fingerprints from it? She began removing the items from it so she could inspect them easier.

"That cellphone looks like it has been stomped on, Commander" Wyatt said.

"It has. Our tech guy tried to salvage the sim card, but the perp went to great lengths to make sure it was smashed beyond recovery of any data. I hope there was nothing on your phone that was irreplaceable, Ms. Summers."

Colleen stopped going through her purse and looked up at him. "It was my work phone. Everything is backed up daily at six p.m. so anything for work was already saved on Friday before I went to the bar. I spoke with my employer this morning and explained how it was stolen and a new one is on its way to me here at the hospital, programmed with the same phone number. The tech department at my company is disabling service to this one."

"We never talked about what you do for a living, Ms. Summers,"

Commander Burns said. "Exactly what is it?"

"I'm currently a pediatric pharmaceutical representative though I have interviewed for a job with one of the top event planners in Chicago. I should hear something later this week. That's why I allowed my employer to send a replacement phone. Until I know whether I have the job or not, I have to keep that number. I don't want to burn any bridges prematurely either."

"Does anyone at your company know you have applied for this job or that you are thinking of leaving?" The commander asked.

"No. I haven't said a word. I've been happy at my job. I just feel that 'dealing pills' for eight years is long enough. Sorry the pharm rep humor. I've paid off my student loans. I have a firm nest egg. I can afford to make a change and I really want to try something different."

"Of course. This was a new angle we hadn't known about until you just mentioned it, so I thought I'd ask. We are still looking and will keep looking even after you go to Montana. Just so you know, we were able to lift some prints off your purse, but nothing has pinged a hit in our criminal database yet."

Colleen nodded, so her guess was right. "Thank you, Commander Burns for your diligence. I do appreciate it."

"What about the artist sketch?" Wyatt asked.

Colleen sucked in her breath as those penetrating eyes flashed through her mind once again.

"We have been running it through facial recognition to see if we get a hit off of it, but nothing yet," Commander Burns explained. "I will keep Wyatt informed in the event we do."

"When that happens, we'll come back from Montana for Colleen to make an identification," Wyatt said.

"Even if it's before I'm ready?" she asked, not liking the thought of being yanked away just to identify the man.

"If you aren't, we'll go back," Wyatt said. "Whatever you need. Don't worry about that now."

"What about doing an identification via telecommunications? It is the electronic age."

Burns arched his brows and smiled. "It might be an option. I'd have to look into it holding up in court and all the legalities, but this is all assuming we'll get a match." He stuffed the evidence bag inside his jacket pocket. "I should get back out there to make sure we're covering as much ground on your case as the others. Have a safe journey if I don't see you again before you leave."

"Thank you, Commander. I appreciate everything you are doing. For me and my friends."

"It's my job, Ms. Summers, but you don't worry about that. You concentrate on getting back on your feet. Hopefully you'll be able to get out of here soon. Any word on that?"

Wyatt shook his head. "I asked the nurse while Colleen was napping and she was going to check with the doctor, but I haven't heard yet. It'd be good to know so I can book a flight."

"Call my office and let my secretary handle the flights for you and see if we can't get you a quicker flight. It's the least the city can do for you," the commander said before leaving.

"He's really been attentive. Do you think he puts as much care in all of his cases?" Colleen said.

"I can't say. I only know that resolving the Pied Piper shooting case is important to him. He has much riding on it. He wants to get a pilot program of the Brotherhood Protectors started here and that is why he has assigned me and my teammates to protect you and your friends. If it all goes well then he'll be able to get the funding he needs to start the Chicago Protection Task Force."

"You mentioned some of this the other day."

"That I did, but I didn't know about the Chicago Protection Task Force then. He only let me know about it when I informed him I was taking you to Montana and he wanted to make sure I was returning to Chicago afterward because he wants me to work with the task force."

"Does that mean you may be moving to Chicago after I return?" Colleen asked.

"It does."

"What about Ruby?" She asked the question before she could stop herself.

He grinned. "She's good humored and goes wherever my job takes me."

Colleen found his response odd. Like Ruby had no say in the matter. What would he do if she wanted to stay in Montana? Would he say Ruby was good humored then?

Smiling to herself, she reached for a tissue and wiped off the powder from the leather before putting her things back into her purse. When she got to her keys, she thought about her apartment.

"Having my purse and keys back means we can go to my apartment tonight if we get out of here and we don't have a flight booked."

"It does."

"My car? Do you think it has been impounded? It was parked along the street near the bar days ago without being moved."

"Give me the make and model and I'll check on the car when I call about the flight reservations." Wyatt said. "I'll also check with Katy about hearing from the doctor on your release."

She gave him the information and he walked toward the door but stopped, when it slid opened.

Katy came in with a box. "This was special delivered for you, Ms. Summers. Good timing because I just received your discharge papers."

"Perfect. I'll go make that call," Wyatt said.

"He's sure in a hurry," Katy said, watching Wyatt leave. The nurse gave a soft sigh as she turned her attention back to her.

Colleen realized she hadn't picked up on how Katy interacted with Wyatt before, but she got it. He was a good-looking man, easy to talk to. Any woman would find it hard not to be attracted to him. Even she was, which was so inappropriate at a time like this. She'd been attacked, almost raped. She knew that. If that gunshot hadn't went off when it did…No. She wasn't letting her thoughts go there.

She returned to what Katy had said. What had she said? Oh yeah. Why was Wyatt in a hurry?

"He's trying to book our flight out of town. *We've* been waiting until we knew I was leaving here to do it."

"Ah. Somewhere nice I hope." She brought the package over to the bed.

"A rehabilitation center for me to deal with my attack. Don't look horrified by it. The place sounds really nice. It's in Montana and Wyatt can't wait to get back there. That is where he's from."

"I'm sure if he is then it must be. Well, let's get you off the IV drip and I'll run through these papers so we can get you out of here. I just need your signature on a few sheets and the rest is recommendations if you start feeling overwhelmed."

Colleen signed where Katy instructed and listened to her review the other sheets of recommendations. Then Katy left to get her a pair of scrubs to wear out of the hospital and a cheap pair of slip on shoes because hers had somehow gone missing from the ER to the room. At least she had the package of underwear that Wyatt had been thoughtful enough to have that detective pick up for her even if she wouldn't have a bra.

By the time Wyatt returned from making the necessary arrangements she was ready to leave the room in her new attire.

"Well, don't you look like a med student," he said when he came into the room.

"I do, don't I?" she tried to smile and make fun with him, but it was hard knowing she'd be leaving this safe haven and going back into the world where that creep who attacked her still lurked.

"The earliest flight I could get is for tomorrow morning. So that means we'll have to crash at your place tonight. Will that be a problem?"

"Not at all. We were going to order pizza anyway, right?" She did manage to smile that time. "And it gives me more time to pack the right type of clothes for Montana. I'm not sure I have what I need for the ranch."

"If you don't, we can always get it there. But if you

have jeans, t-shirts, long-sleeve button ups for when it is chilly, sweat shirts and pants, or sweaters you'll do fine. And the boots we can get in town."

"Boots?"

"You can't wear tennis shoes or slip-on shoes like that on the ranch. You need work boots for mucking out stalls and working with the horses."

"Noted."

"Let's get going."

Colleen picked up her purse and box. "Wait. You never said I'd be mucking out stalls."

He grinned sheepishly. "It goes with ranch life."

"I don't think I'm cut out for ranch life."

"Too late. Tickets are bought and we're already scheduled to be there."

"No fair. You didn't tell me the whole deal."

"Life isn't fair, Ms. Summers."

"You've got that right."

CHAPTER 8

LARGE RANCHES POPULATED the wide-open expanse of two-lane highway as they traveled from the airport toward Eagle Rock, Montana. The view was nothing like Colleen had imagined when Wyatt had talked about wanting to get back to his home since leaving the military other than it was in Montana and that the Brighter Days Rehabilitation Ranch was located there. He hadn't even told her the town was nestled at the base of the Crazy Mountains. She'd found that out on a light up map at the airport while they waited for their luggage. Now that they were here, she was beginning to wonder what appealed to Wyatt about these plains with a few mountains in the distance and the fact he couldn't wait to get back there to Ruby.

Ruby.

She was another enigma that would be known in a very short time. All Colleen knew about Ruby was that she was a good sport and she'd be willing to move to Chicago with Wyatt at the end of this assignment. Colleen silently cringed, looking out the window, and recalled her last boast to Katy about how she and Wyatt were coming to Montana as if the two of them were an item just because Katy had sighed when he'd left the hospital room. Colleen had totally forgotten about Ruby.

Not something she should allow herself to do. Ruby was real and a very big part of Wyatt's life.

"You're quiet," Wyatt said from behind the wheel of the older pale blue pickup truck with white roof that had been waiting on them in the airport parking.

"Taking in the scenery," she replied.

"It's breathtaking for sure. I was awed the first time I saw the hills and plains on my ride from the airport to Eagle Rock."

She smiled at him. "It's so different from Chicago. You can't turn around there without bumping into someone. There isn't a square mile that isn't developed."

"True. But I have been stationed to so many different places in the military that I find each unique in their own way. I adjust to my surroundings. And since I'm retired it's been a good coping tool for these assignments and relocations." He slowed the truck and stopped for a moment, letting it idle in front of a large sign that proclaimed Welcome to Eagle Rock, Montana. "We're here. Do you need to go to town to pick up anything before we go on out to the Brighter Days?"

Colleen shook her head. "I don't think so. Other than the boots."

"We'll get those later. Maybe run to town later this afternoon." Wyatt eased the truck into motion again and they went to where the road forked. He took a right instead of going straight and about half an hour later they pulled up to a big spread that had a large sign at the entrance proclaiming it to be the Brighter Days Rehabilitation Ranch.

They turned off the main road onto a dirt and gravel drive with a wooden split-rail fence row on both sides with a few small trees positioned about every twenty or fifty feet. Wyatt rolled down his window and waved at a few of the riders on horseback as they approached them, though he did not slow down to talk.

Colleen twisted around in her seat when she noticed one of the riders didn't have legs. She decided not to say anything because she knew from what Wyatt had told her that disabled military came here to recover. She just found the fact that the man was able to ride a horse when he had no legs amazing.

"That's Young. He's been at the ranch for years, before I ever joined the Brotherhood Protectors. Don't let his disability fool you. He can out work any one."

She smiled imagining how Young would do that. She was certain she'd soon find out. In the distance she could see a few out buildings and a large barn, up on a slight incline from there sat a sprawling house with a covered front porch.

Between the barn and the ranch house there was a small parking area where a few vehicles were left. Wyatt pulled his truck to a stop next to another truck.

Taking the keys out of the ignition, he turned to her with a big smile. "Hank's here. That means he's brought Ruby over. I can't wait to see her. This is the longest I've been without her."

He opened the door and jumped out of the truck. "Leave your suitcase. I'll come back and get it later. Come on and I'll introduce you to everyone."

Colleen nodded, not sure she was ready to witness a reunion between Wyatt and Ruby after that declaration, but she'd known about her, it wasn't a surprise. What had she been expecting when they got here? That Ruby had left? Where were these crazy thoughts coming from? She wasn't even interested in Wyatt. Hadn't been really interested in anyone in a long time. She'd just been attacked. That alone should make her not want to be close to a man, especially a man as physically fit like Wyatt who could do harm to another person easily. But maybe he was exactly the kind of person she should be attracted to because he could keep her safe. Perhaps that was his appeal. He had made her feel safe ever since he walked into her hospital room.

Wyatt came around and opened her side of the truck door not waiting for her to do it on her own.

"Don't be apprehensive about meeting everyone. I'm sure it's only Hannah and Hank inside, maybe Emma came over with her dad. She and Ruby are pals."

"Okay. Let's meet your people." She slid down from the truck seat to the ground, reaching back for her purse.

Wyatt pointed out their surroundings as they walked the short distance from where they parked toward the ranch house. By the time they came within twenty feet of it, the front door opened and a little girl came running out and a black standard poodle followed her. The poodle ran passed her and straight to Wyatt.

He ran toward the dog, leaving Colleen to walk alone, dropping down to one knee, opening his arms wide. "Ruby!"

Ruby? That's Ruby?

Colleen stopped walking and watched this retired Navy Seal hugging and petting this black standard poodle as she licked him on the neck and face while the little golden-haired girl giggled.

"She's missed you, Wyatt."

"I've missed her too."

"I took real good care of her for you. Daddy says I can get me a puppy of my own now."

"That's great, Emma," Wyatt got to his feet and Ruby jumped up on him, standing on her back legs still licking his neck. He looked over his shoulder. "Colleen, come meet Ruby."

"She's a dog. You never said Ruby was a dog. I thought…"

He pivoted around causing Ruby to jump down and looked at her with his brows furrowed. "Who did you think Ruby was?"

Colleen felt her cheeks warm as she walked closer, closing the gap between them, and she began to laugh, shaking her head at herself. "I thought she was your girlfriend."

"Girlfriend?"

Emma giggled and laughed. "Ruby's a dog, not a girl. That's funny."

Wyatt smiled down at the little girl, ruffling her hair. "Yeah, but totally my fault the way I talked about her, Emma." He looked up at Colleen. "I'm sorry, Colleen. I guess I gave you a false sense of security making you feel I was attached."

A false sense of security? Is that what he thought? Colleen wanted to laugh, but she didn't.

"Clearly it was a misunderstanding by the way you talked about wanting to get back to her," Colleen brushed it off. "I've never felt insecure around you."

"Oh." He nodded, planted his hands square on his hips and smiled at her. "That's good. That's really good."

"Don't give me a reason now to," she added, moving passed him to where Ruby stood beside Emma. She petted the dog on its head and the poodle moved toward her, before she turned her attention to the child. "And who are you? I'm Colleen."

"I'm Emma. My daddy is Wyatt's boss."

"Hank Patterson," Wyatt provided.

"I see. Well, Emma, it's nice to meet you. And thank you for taking care of Ruby so Wyatt could come to Chicago to protect me."

"I love Ruby and she loves me," Emma hugged the dog. "I'd do anything for her."

"I can see that. Do you know what kind of puppy you want to get?"

"Daddy says I can have a smaller Ruby puppy. Wyatt, what does that mean?"

Wyatt laughed and knelt down beside Emma. "There are smaller poodles that don't get as big or stand as tall as Ruby. That is what he wants for you."

"Yeah. I think he said that when I asked. I just forgot. Will you help him find me one? I'm going to miss having Ruby at home now that you are back."

"Sure, I'll help. But you know you can come visit with Ruby anytime."

"How? Daddy won't let me ride my pony off the ranch."

Colleen smiled at the little girl. She was spunky.

"Now Emma, what did I tell you about pestering Wyatt?" a male voice called.

"I wasn't." The little girl planted her hands on her tiny hips and marched toward the front porch where her dad stood with two women. "I was asking. Asking isn't pestering."

The man came down the three wooden steps and scooped the child up in his arms. Emma wrapped her arm around his neck and leaned in to give him a peck on the cheek. She said something and Hank grinned.

Colleen noticed he stood about six feet and he filled out his long-sleeved plaid button up shirt and jeans well, just like Wyatt did. His brown hair was trimmed neatly. The two women followed a short distance behind him.

"I'm Hank Patterson, if you haven't already figured that out," he said offering her his hand. "Welcome to Montana. I see you've already met my outspoken child."

"She's adorable and it's a pleasure. I'm Colleen Summers."

Hank looked passed her. "Wyatt, how's the rest of your team fairing in Chicago?"

"As far as I know they're holding their own. I've not been able to get in touch with them since Saturday, but Hawkeye assures me everything is going well."

"If Hawkeye says so then it must be," Hank agreed. "I packed up part of your gear, just the essentials I thought you'd need while here. Hannah showed me to the cabin where you'd be staying so your things have already been stowed there with Ruby's."

"Thanks, man. I appreciate it. I could have come over later to get it."

"No. You're gonna be needed here," the woman with the long blond hair said. "The patient I asked you to come help with is arriving earlier than expected, so there isn't time for you to even get fully settled in before you have to hit the ground running I'm afraid. As soon as you and Colleen get your bags in from the truck I'll want to have a meeting with you to go over the treatment plan."

"No problem, Hannah." Wyatt leaned toward Colleen. "If you haven't figured it out this is Hannah Kendricks Davila. She is the heart and soul of the Brighter Days ranch. And my new boss while we are here."

"Stop trying to butter me up, Wyatt." Hannah's cheeks flushed. "We're glad to have you here with us, Colleen."

"I'm glad you could make room for me. It's a beautiful place. Wyatt couldn't stop talking about it while we were in Chicago."

"All good, I hope?" Hannah said.

"Of course."

The other female stepped forward. "I'm Ellie Danner. I'll be working with you while you're here."

"Oh, I thought I'd be working with Wyatt." Colleen turned to look at him.

"No. I thought it would be better if you worked with a female counselor. I'll be around. You'll still see me, but you'll spend the majority of your time with Ellie," Wyatt explained.

Colleen nodded.

"Let's get your bag from the truck and get you settled in your room. There's some paperwork to fill out and I bet you need to make a trip to town for boots, am I right?" Ellie glanced down at her shoes and then back up to her face.

"Wyatt and I were going to go later this afternoon," Colleen said.

"I'll take you," Ellie said. "As Hannah said, he's going to be busy this afternoon with his new patient."

"I'll bring in her bag if you want to go on in and start on the paperwork," Wyatt said.

"Sounds good," Ellie agreed. "Shall we, Colleen?"

"Sure." She followed Ellie into the ranch house where they sat down at a large wooden country style table.

Ellie opened a folder and brought out a few sheets of paperwork. "This is your standard in-take papers for any facility. If you don't mind filling these out for us we'll get you officially registered and I'll take you upstairs to your room."

"Wyatt never mentioned how much it was going to cost for me to be here. I'm embarrassed to say I never even asked. I just agreed to come to get away from my bickering divorced parents who couldn't make up their mind which one I should stay with when I was discharged from the hospital, so I made the decision for them."

"There's no need for you to worry about that,

Colleen," Ellie said. "Your fees are covered while you are here. So, don't give it another thought."

Colleen frowned, putting down the pen. "But how? Is Wyatt working here paying for me?"

Ellie shrugged. "I don't know. I just know your file says no charge. Which means it's above my pay grade. I don't ask questions."

"Your ex-military as well?" she asked.

"Ex-special forces."

"Thank you for your service," Colleen said before going back to filling out the forms. She was almost finished when the front door opened and Wyatt came in with Hannah and Ruby.

He sat his duffle and tactical bag beside her suitcase near the sofa and disappeared with Hannah and Ruby into an office, closing the door.

Colleen giggled and shook her head.

"What's so funny?" Ellie asked.

"The poodle. I don't get it. I'd never imagined a Navy Seal having a standard poodle."

"Ruby isn't just a poodle. Didn't Wyatt tell you anything about her?" Ellie asked.

"No. Before we got here, all I knew was that she was possibly a girlfriend he couldn't wait to get back to, the way he kept talking about getting back here to her."

Now Ellie laughed. "I bet that threw you for a loop."

"Yeah. I was stunned when he knelt down and he called out Ruby to the dog."

"She's his PTSD dog. Normally ex-military are

assigned Labradors or German shepherds, but all they had ready was a standard poodle when he was given his. He was put off at first, but Ruby is a sweetheart and she grew on him fast."

"And Emma too."

"That child has been head over heels for that dog since she could walk. Wyatt made the mistake of letting Emma ride Ruby like a pony and the two bonded. He'll be a good dad one of these days."

"Yeah, I saw how he interacted with Emma outside." Colleen signed her name on the last page.

Ellie scooped up the pages and scanned to make sure all were complete before putting them back in the folder. "Let me show you your room upstairs."

Ellie left the file folder in a tray on a console table outside of Hannah's office door. Then she took Colleen's suitcase from her and carried it up the stairs to the second floor.

"There are no locks on the doors other than the standard ones, meaning you can lock the room when you are inside for privacy, but not when you are not. If you have anything you want locked up in a safe for safety reasons, let Hannah know. She has a safe on the premises and can put it in there for you. But otherwise everyone here is trustworthy. Only Hannah and Taz are on the top floor with you. The ranch foreman, Percy Pearson is downstairs, so is Young one of the regulars around here, and of course you'll meet Cookie later at dinner."

"I've heard about him from Wyatt." Colleen followed Ellie into the room she showed her. It was a good size room with a double bed.

"Bathroom is across the hall. Linens in the closet outside the bathroom to the right. Did Wyatt also mention Cookie also likes to let the new client do the cooking for the ranch on his night off?"

Colleen shook her head.

"Well, tonight is not his night off so you are in luck, by the time it is there will be someone new here so you get a reprieve. You might be on dish duty though."

"I can handle that, better than cooking for a crowd."

Ellie lifted the suitcase up on the bed. "Open it up and let me see what you brought so I can tell if you need to pick anything else up while we are in town."

Colleen did as she requested. "Wyatt instructed me on what to bring."

"But he's a guy."

"True," Colleen agreed as she began unpacking and showing Ellie the jeans, tops, sweaters, button ups, sweats, yoga pants and tops, socks.

"I don't see anything for going to a dance."

"A dance?"

Ellie nodded. "There's a dance in town in two weeks. You could always wear jeans, but you might want to wear a blue jean skirt or something. We'll see what we can find you in town. Everyone goes."

"Even Wyatt?"

"Of course, he goes when he isn't on assignment."

. . .

THE DRIVE into town took half an hour and by the time they arrived Colleen's stomach was rumbling. It had been hours since she'd eaten breakfast and the small snack they'd had on the plane was long gone.

"Let me guess, Wyatt didn't stop for lunch before you headed to the ranch from the airport?"

"No. I think he was too anxious to get there and I was too. Food was the last thing on our minds."

"Well, let's grab something at the local diner. We can't have you fainting from low blood sugar while shopping. I don't want him accusing me of not taking care of you on my watch."

"I doubt he'd do that," Colleen said, but she inwardly smiled at the thought that he'd be upset over something happening to her just the same. Then the next moment she chided herself for letting her thoughts run wild. What was wrong with her? Was she crushing on Wyatt Kincaid?

Ellie pulled her small Jeep to a stop outside of the diner and they went inside taking one of the empty booths. The waitress brought over paper menus and two glasses of water.

"Who do you have with you today, Ellie?"

"This is Colleen. A new client at Brighter Days. We're here to get her outfitted for ranch life a little better than she came to town. Colleen, this is Wanda."

"Nice to meet you," Colleen said.

"Welcome to Eagle Rock. I hope you enjoy your stay at Brighter Days. Do you ladies know what you want?"

"Sam's famous burger and rings," Ellie said. "And a tall glass of lemonade."

"Make that times two," Colleen added.

"Easy enough." Wanda removed the menus and left.

Ellie didn't waste a second before she asked her first question. "So, let's get started by you telling me a little about why you are here at Brighter Days. Wyatt told Hannah a little and she jotted it down in the file, but I'd like to hear it from you. I know you decided to come here to get away from your bickering parents, but there has to be more to it than that."

Colleen nodded. "Last Friday night I went out with three of my best friends to a local bar in Chicago. We were getting ready to leave when I decided I needed to visit the ladies. I went alone. Everything was fine until I started to leave. That is when a man broke into the bathroom and attacked me. He beat me, pushing me up against the bathroom stall partition, trapping my arms and hands in front of me while he worked from behind, pushing my clothes…"

Her voice broke and she closed her eyes as hot, stinging tears began rolling down her cheeks. Damn. It was still too soon for her to go into this without breaking into an emotional mess.

Ellie reached for her hand. "I'm sorry. I had no idea my question was going to make you relive that. I thought you would have simply said you were attacked in the ladies, but that your attacker didn't finish what he started."

Colleen reached for a napkin from the table dispenser and wiped at her eyes, then glared across the table at her companion. "If you already knew what happened then why'd you ask?"

"Like I said, I wanted to hear it from you. And clearly this wasn't the place to start with the questions. I appreciate you being so forthcoming with what happened to you. It will make our sessions easier and our time together productive if you can continue to be the same."

Wanda brought their drinks without saying a word.

Colleen nodded, concentrating on opening up the wrapper on her straw. "I don't know why I told you about the attack."

"Has it been bothering you?"

"No. They can't find the guy, at least they haven't. They had me give them a sketch of what I recalled seeing of him."

"That's good. I'm sure they'll be able to find him off of it in time."

Colleen shrugged, "Maybe, but it wasn't him."

"It wasn't?"

"No. It was a pair of eyes that have haunted me for years."

Wanda sat their food in front of them as well as a new bottle of ketchup. "Enjoy. I'll be back to check on you."

"Thanks," Ellie said. She prepared her burger and took a bite, chewing thoughtfully before she spoke again.

"About the sketch, have you told Wyatt about the eyes?"

"Only that I see them when I close my eyes. Which I do. It isn't a lie."

"Why do you believe you described them for the sketch artist instead of the attacker?"

Colleen reached for her lemonade, drinking from it for several seconds before she finally looked up at Ellie. "I don't know. The artist took me back to that time in the bathroom and when he was finished with the drawing that was what he had for his result."

"I see." Ellie popped a golden ring in her mouth and chewed. "Well, we'll figure it out in another session. We have plenty of time to discover why those eyes were what came to mind. And don't worry, what you tell me in our sessions are private. I won't be sharing it with Wyatt."

Colleen fixed her burger and took a bite, her teeth sinking into the patty like it was butter. She moaned at the flavor and she heard Ellie giggle at her.

"Range raised to plate makes all the difference. No processing."

"Oh my."

She sank into the booth seat and savored every morsel of the burger and rings, taking a refill on the lemonade when Wanda came by. She was even tempted by the offer of blueberry alamode pie for dessert, but Ellie reminded her that Cookie would have dinner waiting on them when they returned to the ranch.

"We'll come earlier in the day next time," Colleen assured the waitress as they settled their checks before walking across the street to the general store which carried groceries, clothing, as well as footwear.

"Wyatt said I needed boots for mucking out stalls," Colleen said walking the aisle of cowboy boots that were too fancy looking for wearing in a barn. She reached for a cute pair that were a buckskin, cream and tan combination in her size.

Ellie put the boots back on the shelf. "Then you need to follow me to the rubber boot section. They work best because they protect your feet in all types of weather and can be hosed off when you get into mud and muck."

"I liked those."

"Maybe for the town dance, but not working on the ranch."

As they went to find the rubber boots Colleen spotted a rack of blue jean skirts with a ruffled trim around the hem. "That's cute."

"Again, something to consider for the town dance," Ellie said. She grabbed a matching top off another rack and handed it to her. "With this."

Colleen put the two pieces together and imagined herself wearing it, even though the skirt did not go all the way down to her ankles, but with the boots, only her knees and a small portion of her shins would show. That wouldn't be bad.

"Come on, time's wasting."

She hung the items back on the racks and hurried to catch up with Ellie. Soon they found her the right size of rubber boots, a dozen pairs of boot socks and then they went back to the blue jean skirt and top to find her size for the dance and then she found her size in the cowboy boots. "I'm not leaving here without them."

"Then get them," Ellie agreed. "While you are at it, there is one last item you must have out on the ranch. A straw hat to protect your head."

Ellie looked through the selection hanging on a pole until she found the one she thought was right and then she planted it on Colleen's head. "How does that feel? What do you think it looks like on you?"

Colleen inspected herself in the mirror and decided she liked it. The fit wasn't too snug either. "It's good."

"Since we're going into summer I'd suggest you go with a straw hat instead of a felt one. More breathing room."

They went to the register and she made her purchase before heading back across the street with three shopping bags full to where Ellie parked her Jeep. Their conversation on the way back to the ranch was light for which Colleen was thankful. She was beginning to feel the after effects of traveling across the Midwest this morning and she didn't feel she could handle getting into anything too heavy this evening. She was looking forward to a hot shower and maybe sitting around the firepit she saw behind the ranch house earlier from her bedroom window. She thought it would be nice to sip coffee as the sun dipped low in the sky and lounge back there.

She mentioned it to Ellie.

"Love to join you, but I have some paperwork to catch up on tonight. Maybe another time?"

"Oh, sure." Colleen went into the house and up to her room. She unpacked her shopping bags, hung up her new skirt and blouse, as well as her other clothes that she wasn't putting in one of the four drawers of the chest. Then she put her boots in the closet. She took a shower and dressed in clean clothes, making herself presentable for the evening meal.

When she came down for dinner she looked for Wyatt, but he wasn't around. She sat with Hannah and was introduced to the other clients residing on the ranch as well as the staff members who were eating with them that evening.

Instead of going out to the firepit she went to her room early disappointed. If this was the way things were going to be maybe it would have been better to have stayed in Chicago. She'd have at least had Wyatt all to herself there.

CHAPTER 9

WYATT WALKED Ruby one last time before turning in for the night. He stopped outside the ranch house at the back and looked up where a lone light burned golden in a partially drawn curtained window. He wondered if that was Colleen's room. He hated deserting her today, but Hannah had been right. He'd had to hit the ground running on this assignment. The file was a complicated one on his client and he had to be up to speed tomorrow when the guy arrived.

He'd had choice words with Hannah earlier that afternoon for allowing him to bring Colleen here once he'd gotten into this guy's file and discovered he'd been falsely accused not once, but twice of sexual misconduct by fellow female personnel. No formal charges were brought against him, because there was never convicting evidence.

"Those are all allegations that were not proven. I

cannot turn any soldier away from this facility because he was accused of something like that. Especially when we have one of the best Traumatic Brain Injury programs available to medically discharged military. Plus, he doesn't remember any of it. His therapist at Walter Reed went over his case with a fine-tooth comb making sure he wasn't a threat to anyone before they discharged him."

Wyatt had paced her office. "You still should have told me."

"I have it under control," Hannah assured him. "Ellie is aware of this guy's track record and the sensitivity of Colleen's condition. She'll make sure that when you are working in the stables to stay away so that they do not cross paths. But both are clients here, Wyatt. Each deserve privacy for their treatments and whatever Tate Hackles may or may not have done while he was serving in the military is in his past. Those records were sealed. We only know about them because of his TBI and how he may not be in total control now."

"Or he could be a repeat offender. We'll just have to wait and see."

Hannah had frowned. "Let's not go there."

"I'm not letting him near Colleen. We'll eat our meals in his private cabin. I'll make an excuse that it is best for his program if he asks why he isn't socializing with the other clients at first."

"That's your call as his therapist."

He held up a finger, but he'd been unable to point it

at Hannah. "If something happens to Colleen while we're here I'll hold you personally responsible."

"I'll hold myself responsible. I've discussed this with Taz and he's got your six on this. He'll be watching in the background."

Wyatt nodded. "I'll be taking my dinner in my cabin tonight. I still have lots to plan for tomorrow."

"Of course."

He'd left her office and snapped his finger at Ruby who'd waited for him outside the door. They'd went back to his cabin leaving only to get his tray when Cookie had called that victuals were ready or for Ruby to do her business.

Now he was wondering if he overreacted. But his job was to protect Colleen not bring her to a place that was going to put her in harm's way, albeit unknowingly.

"Don't tell me you're pining over her?" Ellie Danner's humor filled voice coming out of the dark night before she came into view of the moonlight caused him to jump. "Sorry, didn't mean to startle you."

"I was thinking about my new client," Wyatt replied.

"Ah, yeah, that is a tricky situation."

"Hannah let me come out here and get blind sighted with this?"

"You got her all wrong." Ellie crossed her arms over her chest and stood at ease.

"Do I?"

"She needed a counselor and with Cole Ramsey

away for the unforeseeable future traveling with his partner Vanessa, she couldn't call him back for one case, but this guy got a glowing report from Leigha Nipton and you know what a stickler she is."

Wyatt nodded remembering the nurse at Walter Reed that had talked to him about coming to Montana to work with Hank Patterson. She'd been tough as nails on him when he was recovering, but once he was ready to be released she'd turned sweet as molasses, as his momma used to say.

"That wasn't in the file."

"Not everything has to be. Hannah called and talked to Nipton after she learned the woman had been his nurse during a conversation with one of his doctors at Walter Reed."

"It sounds like Hannah vetted this guy thoroughly before she agreed to let him come here." *Shit!* He felt like an ass for not trusting Hannah's judgement call, but he also knew a snake was always a snake until he showed his fangs. Therefore he'd allow Hackles to prove himself trustworthy.

"Did you doubt that when you saw the highlighted and flagged passages in his file? Taz suffered from TBI too and he still deals with a little confusion at times even after so many years post-trauma, though he doesn't like to talk about it. He does the exercises to get him over the rough patches and move forward. Just like you deal with your PTSD."

Wyatt nodded. "That doesn't mean I won't be

watching Hackles like a hawk until I'm sure he isn't a threat."

"None of us will let our guard down around him. For Colleen or any of the other females at the ranch." Ellie patted him on the shoulder. "Get some sleep. We've got a big day ahead tomorrow."

Wyatt gave one last look up at the window on the second floor and saw the light had gone out. Ellie was right. It was time to get some sleep. "Let's go, Ruby."

COLLEEN HAD FINISHED breakfast and was sipping coffee while observing one of the stable hands named Kid talk to another client about working with the horses down at the stables. She found the conversation interesting and she'd heard the two of them talking the night before along the same lines. Kid was quite convincing in his spiel about what to do to handle the horses, even for a novice like the client.

"You want to go for a walk?" Ellie sat a bottle of water in front of her. "I like to start each morning with a good walk after breakfast. It gets the fresh mountain air in my lungs and works any tension from the night before out of my system."

Colleen rose from the table and grabbed the bottle of water, following Ellie out the side door. "It's good you came when you did or I might have followed Kid down to the stables. After listening to him, I was certain I could have tackled brushing and saddling a horse all on my own even though I've never been around one."

"I'm sure he'd have put you through your paces down there if you had. But you'd have needed your rubber boots."

She looked down at her white tennis shoes as they followed the split-railed fence row where a nice foot trail had been worn. "True. Wouldn't want to ruin these even if I've had them six months."

"And they still look like they're out of the box?"

"They practically are. I don't wear them often in my line of work. We rarely have dress down days. So, I wear them in my apartment sometimes and occasionally when I go out with my friends."

"What is it that you do?" Ellie asked.

"I'm a pediatric pharmaceutical representative."

"Do you like doing that?"

Colleen shrugged. "It worked for me until a couple of months ago and that is when I made the decision to start looking for something different. There is only so many ways you can convince a doctor to give a new drug a try or to continue using a drug before it becomes old and I had reached my expiration point. I've interviewed with an events planner in Chicago. I actually have a second interview pending that I'm waiting to hear more about. So, I hope you don't mind that I have my cellphone with me during our sessions."

"Thanks for letting me know." Ellie cut across the pasture land toward a shade tree and a wooden picnic table near the house. "What made you decide to apply for a job with an events planner? That seems to be a huge pendulum swing from drug rep to events."

"I like throwing parties. I was always on the planning committee in my sorority. I don't know why I didn't think of it as a career move after graduation, but the drug rep has helped me pay off my student loans and build a good nest egg because I have lived frugally for the most part."

Ellie nodded as they reached the tree and Colleen noticed there was a notebook waiting on the table. She took a seat on the bench on one side while Ellie sat on the opposite.

Ellie wasted no time opening up the notebook and uncapping the pen lying beside it. She studied Colleen a moment before she spoke.

"When we were at the diner yesterday you jumped right in and told me about your attack in the lady's room at the bar that led to Wyatt being assigned to protecting you. Today, I'd like you to tell me how that attack made you feel."

Colleen almost laughed at the question, but knew it was a legitimate question and she didn't find the subject a laughing matter even though the answer was obvious.

"How do you think it made me feel? I felt violated. He broke into the bathroom, he busted my lip when he backhanded me, he gave me a blackeye. All I see when I close my eyes at night is a pair of eyes haunting me, those eyes that I can't get out of my mind again."

Ellie wrote that in her notebook. "Tell me more about those eyes. You said they were the eyes that you described for the sketch artist, but they weren't the eyes of the attacker at the bar. Who do those eyes belong to?"

"I...I." Colleen stammered, watching Ellie scribble in her notebook. "They're piercing eyes. They haunt my sleep."

Then she stopped writing and looked up at Colleen. "A pair of eyes cannot hurt you. The attack you sustained on Friday night is over."

Her words were warm and her voice was gentle, almost soothing. Colleen found herself hanging onto every word she spoke and when she laid her pen down and covered her hand with a comforting squeeze, she didn't pull away.

"Your bruising is slowly going away around your eye. The busted lip is almost unnoticeable. You were not raped which is a blessing. The memory of the assault will eventually fade away if you allow it. Talking about it will help. Not keeping your feelings bottled up inside will help."

"He took everything from me. He took my dignity. My vi..." Colleen stopped herself before she said the word on the tip of her tongue. "My identity. He stole everything when he ran away with my purse. How can I feel safe going back to Chicago until he is caught?"

She hugged herself, not believing she almost let it slip about the actual rape, she never talked about it. Ellie's kindness was a slippery slope she had to be careful around or she'd find herself opening up.

Maybe it was time.

No. She couldn't risk anyone finding out. He'd warned her what would happen if they did.

Ellie stared at her for a moment, placing the top of the pen against her lips as she watched her closely. The silence between them stretched on until Colleen began to feel uncomfortable. Had the counselor picked up on her blunder? Did she realize what she had started to say?

Finally, Ellie put the pen back on her table. "I'm sure the police are working on finding the man who did this to you. You did receive your belongings back before leaving town. It was in the report Wyatt filed on your background."

"Yes, I did, but Commander Burns didn't sound hopeful of catching the man who attacked me."

"He probably didn't want to give you false hope."

"Maybe." Colleen got up and walked around the tree, coming back to stand with her back against it behind where she'd been sitting. "Besides feeling violated I am angry."

"Who are you angry at?

"At the man who picked me to assault. Why me? Why not any other woman in the bar? Why did he have to follow after me when I went to the lady's room? Why not follow someone outside of the bar? Why?"

"Those are all valid questions. And let's consider what would have happened if that man had followed someone outside of the bar. You were there with your friends if I recall. When you went to the lady's room what happened with them?"

Colleen frowned and shook her head. "Oh no. You are not going make me suggest that I'd rather he have attacked Jules because she left the bar while I went to the lady's room."

Ellie held up her hands, palms out. "I am only asking you to explore the options you set forth in your question 'why me' scenario. Why not someone else? If not you, then Jules, it seems."

Colleen hung her head and slammed the heel of shoe against the tree trunk. "That's not fair."

"It's not fair that it happened to anyone. That is what's not fair."

A brief silence engulfed them.

Colleen avoided making eye contact with Ellie. Instead she worried the toe of her shoe along the smooth exterior of an exposed root of the tree.

"Okay," Ellie finally said. "I think we need to take a small break. It's getting pretty warm out here and we're about the lose our shade as the sun hits midday. We can move to my cabin and work there for the afternoon. I can have Cookie send lunch of sandwiches and a large pitcher of lemonade over for us if you want?"

She nodded before finally pushing away from the tree. In the distance she thought she saw Ruby running between one of the cabins to another. Then she saw Wyatt walking with someone, assuming it was his new client.

"When will we be working in the stables?"

"We're scheduled there tomorrow morning after breakfast so wear your boots."

Colleen nodded.

WYATT GOT TATE HACKLES settled into his private cabin after showing him around the main ranch house. They took seats in the small living room. Wyatt sat in the easy chair and Tate on the sofa. Ruby sat beside the easy chair on Wyatt's left.

"I've scheduled you to have your meals in your cabin for the first week to give you time to adjust to your new surroundings."

"Thanks. With the headaches I have late afternoon into early evening I think that is best," the man said.

Wyatt studied him for a moment feeling like he'd met him before, but couldn't place where. There was something very familiar about Tate Hackles he couldn't shake.

"Do you mind if I ask where you have been stationed? I'm wondering if we may have crossed paths in theater? You look familiar to me for some reason.

Maybe we've passed one another in mess hall or something."

Tate grinned. "Wouldn't that be funny?" He rattled off a list of locations but Wyatt hadn't been to any of them, however he didn't let on.

"I hate not being able to place a face and now with TBI, I can't even recall so many things that I should know."

"We're going to work on that while you are here so that won't be an issue for you. Let's start with a breathing exercise to help you relax. Close your eyes, letting your mind go blank. Deep breath in through the nose and slowly exhale. Good. Now, raise your shoulders up and rotate them slowly backwards and let them gently fall, pushing away the anxiety. Inhale another deep cleansing breath, hold it for a count a two and exhale through the mouth."

"Do you honestly think breathing is going to help my tension?" Tate asked.

Ruby tilted her head and made a noise. Wyatt patted her on her side to calm her down after his client's rude outburst. "It's okay girl."

He turned his attention to Tate. "It won't if you're going to have that attitude. Nothing we do in our sessions will work unless you have a positive attitude and are open to it."

"Sorry man. I'll try to be more approachable with these techniques. It's just these headaches I have make me so damn irritable all the time and then I get angry for no reason."

"That's all part of traumatic brain injury. I'm going to have you talk to Taz Davila, he's Hannah's husband. He has TBI. He dealt with much of the same anger issues and headaches when he first came to Brighter Days."

"No shitting?"

Wyatt got him talking about his accident and what he remembered. He told him about his own accident in Afghanistan to build rapport with him. By the time lunch came Tate needed a break so Wyatt took his container of food and drink back to his own cabin and allowed his client to rest for a couple of hours. This would also give him time to find Hannah and apologize for thinking the worst.

He saw her slipping on a pair of work gloves and heading toward the stables when he left Hackles cabin. "Hey, Hannah, wait up."

Ruby took off galloping across the expanse of ground between them and nuzzled the woman's hand.

Hannah stopped and turned. "Do you need something?"

"To eat crow. I'm guessing that is what Cookie sent from the kitchen."

She grinned. "I wouldn't know what he's serving you today. Unless you pissed him off. Then you very well may be eating crow."

"I overreacted about Hackles. After meeting him he

does seem like a harmless client. I'm not letting my guard down completely, but after talking with Ellie she made me see things a little clearer and I was being unfair to you. I was in protector mode."

"Which you should be. That is your number one job for Colleen."

"But I've known you long enough to know you'd never intentionally put anyone here on the ranch at risk by bringing a client here that could harm them," Wyatt went on. "And for that I am truly sorry."

Hannah smiled. "I accept your apology. Like I told you yesterday, Taz has your six on this. Hank is only a phone call away if we need him. Ellie will get Colleen away from here if she needs to until we give her the all clear. Safety measures are in place."

Wyatt nodded and let out a deep breath. "Thanks again for looking out for her. I won't keep you from your destination. Ruby and I were headed back to my cabin for lunch while Tate rests after our morning session. It gave him a headache."

"His doctors said he still is suffering from those. Go easy for the first few days with him. Let him build up to longer sessions if you need to see if that will help keep the headaches at bay. Especially if the breathing techniques are not working."

"Will do." Wyatt took a few steps backward and whistled for Ruby to follow him before he pivoted into an about face and headed in the direction of his cabin.

CHAPTER 10

COLLEEN SLIPPED her rubber boots on and headed downstairs to meet up with Ellie after breakfast, ready for her first experience in the stables, but her counselor wasn't there yet. She joined in the conversation with Kid and the client from the day before who were finishing up their breakfast, learning the man's name was Stefan and he'd been here a week. He had a prosthetic hand and he didn't believe he could be useful in the stables, but Kid was proving him wrong.

"I've never been in a stable before," Colleen told them, trying not to stare at his hand. It was hard to believe it wasn't real, the prosthesis looked natural in coloring and design. Even the fingernails looked real. "So, don't think you are the worst person to work down there today. I'll be coming as soon as Ellie gets here."

Kid and Stefan chuckled.

"You'll be welcome, Colleen," Kid said. "Even if you aren't military."

She sucked in her breath. "How could you tell?"

"It takes one to know one," Stefan explained. "And you ain't got the look."

She laughed at that. "No. I'm a civilian who was lucky enough to be allowed to come here for the rehab I need."

"Then you'll get it and more," Kid added. He rose from the table and picked up his dirty dishes. "Come on Stefan those horses are not going to feed themselves."

"Alright. See you down there."

"See you soon."

Colleen tapped her finger nails on the deserted polished table and wondered what was taking Ellie so long. Was she supposed to be taking her morning walk before they went down to the stable? It wasn't mentioned when they parted company yesterday.

The door to Hannah's office opened and Ellie emerged with Hannah one step behind her followed by a dark looking man. Was that Taz? She'd heard about Hannah's husband how he was dark and handsome, but he'd been away on a job and had not taken the evening meal with them the last two nights. He certainly was built like Wyatt. Was he ex-military too? That certainly would explain why he looked like the total package in those snug, black jeans and black t-shirt, dark aviator glasses pushed up on his head. He slipped into a shoulder holster and slipped his firearm into the pouch before putting on a black jacket and zipping it up before giving Hannah a quick kiss.

Yes, that had to be Taz.

"Sorry to keep you waiting." Ellie smiled as she approached. "We had to close out a case from last week. But I'm all yours now. Shall we head out for a short walk on our way to the stables?"

"Um hum," Colleen murmured still watching as Taz left the house.

Ellie turned and saw where her eyes were trained. "You haven't met Davila yet. He's a Brotherhood Protector like Wyatt. Did you know that?"

She shook her head.

"That's how he met Hannah. He was assigned here to keep her safe and to rehab after leaving Walter Reed for his TBI. But mainly to protect Hannah from the threats she was receiving."

"Ellie, don't bring up that story of how Taz and I met. Colleen will believe that every woman who ends up with a Brotherhood Protector has to have been in danger."

"But they kinda do, don't they, Hannah?" Ellie asked.

"Okay, they do," Hannah admitted.

Colleen giggled. "It's okay. I get it. They're darn

charming is what it is. We can't help but find them attractive."

"Exactly!" Hannah said. "I know of a few charming horses waiting for your care."

"We're going," Ellie said.

KID HANDED Colleen a pitch fork and showed her a stall that had been mucked out. "Stefan has already removed the messy hay. I want you to put in a fresh layer of hay for the horse from this wagon. Spread it even in the stall."

"Sounds easy enough," she said, putting on the work gloves Ellie had given her on the way down to the stables.

"Really, Kid? Is that what you're calling it these days?" Ellie questioned him. "Messy hay instead of the manure pile?"

Kid shrugged. "It seemed more fitting for a lady."

Colleen giggled as she started spreading the hay. He thought she was a lady. That made her feel good in these rubber boots and work gloves, her oldest pair of broken in jeans and old t-shirt. Yet to him she still looked like a lady.

By the time she finished spreading hay into four stalls her back and arm muscles were screaming in protest. She knew the task wasn't as easy as it sounded and she wasn't cut out for working on a ranch. Dragging around her suitcase of pill samples was light work compared to this.

She stopped, stuck the pitch fork in the nearest clump of hay and removed her work gloves, sticking them in her back-jean pocket. She wiped the perspiration off her forehead with her right forearm and noticed Kid and Stefan watching her.

"What? Did I do something wrong?" she asked.

"No. You've done great," Kid said. "I asked you to do one stall and you did all four. It was hard for Stefan to keep ahead of you."

"Really?" Colleen felt the smile spread across her face.

"Are you sure you don't want to work down here with us every day?" Stefan asked.

She laughed. "I think Ellie has other plans for me."

"Indeed, I do." Ellie appeared in the wide-open stable doorway. "I hope you are bone tired and ready to relax for a talk session."

"Am I ever. It has felt good working down here, but I am ready for a break." Colleen looked at Kid and Stefan. "If you both think you can get along without me."

Kid looked at Stefan and then back at her. "It'll be hard, but I think we can manage."

"Thank you, guys," Ellie said and they went back up to the ranch house. "I'll get lunch for us while you run up to your room and clean up."

"That sounds heavenly. I could use a quick hot shower. I used muscles I didn't know I had back there."

"This place will do that to you," Ellie said. "I remember when I first arrived and was helping with my first client go through her paces down at the stables. I thought I was in great shape coming from special-ops, but working with horses can teach you a thing or two. And you only dealt with putting out fresh hay today. Wait until Kid has you dealing with the 'messy hay' as he is calling it just for you, his lady."

Colleen rolled her eyes taking the three steps up the front of the ranch house in stride, stopping at the top to remove her rubber boots. "I thought that was sweet of him to think of me as a lady. Don't tease him. He comes across as a little shy, except when he's talking about horses."

"Kid is used to me teasing him." Ellie opened the door. "He wouldn't know how to act if I didn't anymore."

"I won't be long," Colleen called and hurried up the stairs to her room. She grabbed her toiletries and a change of clothes before going across the hall to the bathroom.

When she returned downstairs she saw Ruby sitting at the bottom of the staircase as if she was waiting for her. But why would Wyatt's PTSD dog be doing that?

"What are you doing here, girl?"

"Because I'm here." Wyatt stood from the armchair that sat against the wall which is why she hadn't noticed him before. "She heard you coming and went to wait for you."

Colleen gulped. It had only been two days since she had seen him, but if felt like a lifetime. He looked so hot in his usual tight, black t-shirt and black cargo pants. She licked her lips because her mouth suddenly felt so dry she was having trouble forming words. Reaching for the banister, she steadied herself.

"Wh-What are you doing here? I thought you had a client that was going to keep you busy?"

"I do, but he is dealing with headaches associated with his traumatic brain injury and he has to take naps often to help with them. We are doing relaxation exercises, but he is still fresh out of Walter Reed and sleeping is the best medicine right now."

"Well, his loss is my gain it seems if we can spend a few moments together. I'm glad to see you. It seems odd not to spend time with you every day. I was about to have lunch with Ellie."

"Actually, you're having lunch with me and Ruby."

"I am?" Colleen smiled. "Did you arrange this?"

"I did. I feel bad for bringing you out here and practically abandoning you into the hands of a stranger because I'm working with someone else. That wasn't the way you thought it would be, I'm sure. Not after spending twenty-four hours a day with me every day since you entered the hospital. I'm supposed to be protecting, not abandoning, you."

"Wyatt." She took the remaining steps down,

petting Ruby on the head, giving her hand something to do. "I'm working with a former special force operative. I think Ellie has protection down if I need it. Plus, there is Taz and how many other ex-soldiers on this ranch. This place is covered almost better than Fort Knox."

"But they are not assigned to protect you. I am."

She nodded and looked over at the large table where the meals were eaten. Their lunch was waiting and she was starving. "Let's not squabble. I'm hungry. What about you?"

WYATT HADN'T EXPECTED SEEING Colleen again to make him feel like he'd been sucker punched in the gut. It had only been two days, but it might as well have been two months the way his groin had sprang to life upon seeing her standing on the stairs smelling all showered fresh with wet tendrils of hair at the nape of her neck. He really didn't know what had come over him. He'd not reacted this way to her when he'd been protecting her in the hospital. Why now? Was it because she was back on her feet or had it been the fact that she'd thought Ruby was his girlfriend, indicating she might be interested? Who was he kidding she couldn't be, could she? Not after the assault?

However, all sane thoughts went south with the lightning jolt when she took his hand and led him over to the table. His breathing became labored and it was hard to focus on what she was saying as he watched her cute bottom move side to side with each step. He soon regained control of his senses as they sat at the table and decided to keep a respectable distance between them, gulping his tea before refilling his glass.

"Is counseling with Ellie going well?" he asked, thankful his voice didn't crack.

Colleen nodded. "We've had a couple of sessions now and I believe so. She wants me to talk it out and not keep it bottled up. She said that is the main thing to help me get over my assault."

"Are you still having the nightmares of those eyes?"

"Yes."

He had the urge to lay his hand on hers, but suppressed it. "I'm sure that will fade in time too."

"I hope."

"Listen, Ellie has asked for me to get Commander Burns to send the sketch artist's drawing to her in email. Are you okay with her having that sketch? I wanted to ask before I got it for her."

Colleen laid down her dill pickle that she was about to take a bite into, wiped her hands on the paper napkin and swiveled to face him in the chair. "If she believes it will help with my sessions then I guess it can't hurt."

"Good. I'll get in it after lunch."

Her leg brushed against his when she swiveled back

around and it sent another jolt through him letting him know they weren't far enough apart. Why was he having this reaction to her today? He'd never done this with an assignment before and he wasn't about to start now. He instantly made up his mind to ignore this physical attraction, even if it killed him.

CHAPTER 11

"I HOPE you don't mind, but I asked Wyatt to get me a copy of the sketch artist's drawing," Ellie said as soon as Colleen got settled on the couch for their session that afternoon.

"He mentioned it at lunch. He wanted my permission to get it for you."

"Oh. Well I was going to mention it when we started our session."

Colleen nodded. "It's fine. Not sure what you want it for."

"I thought we could look at it and talk about why those eyes haunt you when you close your eyes."

"I see." She hugged the couch pillow to her chest and kicked off her tennis shoes so she could tuck her feet under her.

"I believe it will help you get over it." Ellie smiled. "I

was proud of your work at the stables this morning. I hope your lunch with Wyatt went well?"

"It did. A very nice surprise. Thank you if you had anything to do with arranging it."

"Just a tiny part. I got you there. He did the rest, down to ordering the food." Ellie opened up her notebook and propped her feet on the end of the rustic coffee table, laying it on her bent knees. "Did he happen to ask you to the town dance?"

"No. You are the only one on the ranch that has talked about this dance. Are you sure it's happening?"

"Of course, it is. There's still time. Don't worry. If he doesn't we'll go stag."

"I'm not worried."

"Let's do a quick breathing exercise to relax us before we start our session. Close your eyes and breath in deep through the nose and exhale out through the mouth. Breath in again and exhale slowly. Breath in again and exhale and tell me about the night in the bar? You're getting ready to leave, but make a stop in the lady's room."

Eyes closed, Colleen shook her head. "No."

"It's okay," Ellie said. "You're safe. No one can hurt. What happened is in the past. We're just revisiting a memory. Use the pillow you are clutching as a grounding tool. Squeeze it for comfort. Now take a deep, cleansing breath in and slowly exhale it out. Can you tell me what you see, Colleen?"

"A dark figure coming through the door at me. He hits me, drawing blood. A metallic taste fills my mouth as I'm slammed against a hard-plastic wall."

"Okay, stop. Tell me about the dark figure. What does he look like?"

"A dark blob."

"What color hair?"

"I don't know. Brown I think."

"What's the shape of his eyes?"

"I don't know. It all happened so fast. I didn't get a good look at him. He hit me with such force it turned me around and I banged into the partition."

"Then why do the eyes haunt you?" Ellie asked.

"I told you before the eyes aren't his," Colleen said through gritted teeth sitting ram rod straight.

"Are you certain, Colleen? The mind can play tricks. You may not realize you saw more than you did in that instance he came at you. You may think the eyes are from another time in your past, but could be from this attack."

She shook her head and squeezed the pillow tight. "No. No. I know those eyes. There's nothing you can say to make me doubt myself."

"Then how do you know those eyes?" Ellie asked.

Colleen stared at her, breathing labored. Did she dare answer that question or not? Knots formed in her stomach at the mere thought of talking about those eyes and why she knew them. Bile threatened to rise and she gasped for air. She clutched the front of her shirt trying to pull it away from her skin to allow a cool breeze to get to her.

"Okay we need to take a break. You don't have to answer that right now."

Ellie put down her notebook and ran into the little kitchenette. She returned with a glass of water for her. "Try to drink this."

She gulped the water and was surprised she was able to keep it down. "I'm sorry. I can't tell you about those eyes. Something horrible will happen to me if I do."

Ellie sat down on the edge of the couch beside her. "What do you mean something will happen to you, Colleen? Have you been threatened?"

She nodded, despite her resolve to keep silent.

"Did your attacker threaten you?"

"Yes," she whispered so softly it was barely audible.

"Have you told anyone else about this?"

"Only you."

"Finish the water, relax, bathroom is down the hall if you need it. I will be right back. I need to run to the main house and check if that email came through yet."

"Okay."

Ellie handed her a square box of tissues before she left the cabin.

. . .

WYATT SAT at the kitchen table in his cabin going over Hackles' file, filling in his session notes from that morning. Progress with his client wasn't moving as fast as he would like, but each case went at their own speed. Clearly Hackles wasn't ready to leave Walter Reed as his doctors thought.

Urgent knocking pounded on his cabin door and Ruby immediately started barking. He tried to calm her down as he got up to answer it but the dog would not be appeased until the door was opened.

"Ellie, what is wrong?"

"Did you know Colleen was threatened?" She pushed into the cabin. "Of course, you didn't. She didn't tell you, because she just told me."

"Whoa. Whoa. Slow down here. What do you mean? Threatened? By who?"

"That is what we have to find out. By her present attacker or by the owner of the eyes that haunts her at night."

Wyatt felt his gut tighten into a knot. "Aren't they the same?"

Ellie shook her head. "No. She admitted to me the day she arrived those eyes in the drawing weren't from her attacker in the bathroom, but from someone else."

"Holy crap!" He shut the door. "I have to let Commander Burns know that if he gets a match on those eyes it won't be for the attack at the Pied Piper, but for something else. Has she told what?"

"No. I just know she is petrified to identify or talk about those eyes in detail because of being threatened."

Wyatt leaned his hands on the back of the couch and stared across the cabin. "But she is safe here. No one knows her. These attacks happened in Chicago and she's in Montana now. We have to make her see this."

"Come back to my cabin with me and talk to her. I'm going to go to the main house and check email for the sketch."

Wyatt looked at his watch. "I have a session with my new client. If he's awake."

"Push it back an hour. Colleen needs you."

"I'll be there if I can."

Ellie left without another word and Wyatt let out a curse. How could he have not seen this when they were in Chicago? He'd been with Colleen twenty-four hours a day. She'd never given any indication about being threatened. Nor that the eyes in the drawing were not of the attacker in the lady's room. Why would she keep these two important details from him? Unless she didn't trust him.

No, that couldn't be the reason. Surely, she did trust him. You can't feel safe around someone and not trust them. Can you?

He went over to the table and closed up Hackles' file and grabbed his notebook, prepared to head over to the man's cabin to see if he was ready for their session which he silently prayed he wouldn't. He left

Ruby in the cabin. She didn't like it, but there was no reason to take her with him if he was just going to be coming back before heading over to Ellie's.

Knocking on Hackles' cabin door, he waited a few moments between knocks before he rapped again and he finally heard movement inside.

The door swung open and the man shaded his eyes with one hand from the bright light of the day. "Sorry, I was still lying down. Is it time for our session already?"

"It is, if you are up for it?" Wyatt said.

"I think the headache has turned into a migraine," Hackles moved out of the doorway for him to come inside.

"Do you get them often?"

"Only after my injury. I have a prescription, but it will knock me out. If I take it we won't be able to work this afternoon."

"Would we be able to work with the migraine?

"No."

"Then take your prescription and I'll check on you later today. We can have a short late session if we need to make up for it or start fresh tomorrow. Your health is the most important part of this experience."

"Thanks man for understanding."

"No problem, Tate. If you need anything we do have a medic on staff here. Just let us know."

Wyatt left worried about his client. He wasn't sure he knew what to do to help him with his situation. He needed to talk to Taz about his own experience with

TBI and see if he could give him some pointers on how to deal with what Hackles was going through.

That was what was on his mind when he walked back into his cabin to leave his notebook and retrieve Ruby. He also picked up his secure cell and gave Commander Burns a call. He had to walk close to the main house near the internet connection for it to work, but he got the call to go through. Spotty towers. That was what he hated about Montana, but what could you do?

His call went straight to voice mail so he left a message and turned around and called the office line talking briefly with the Commander's admin assistant. She took a message as well, but was not forthcoming about the whereabouts of the Commander.

He ended the call and walked to Ellie's cabin with Ruby galloping along beside him. She stopped to potty and every so often to sniff the ground and then ran to catch up with him. He knocked once on the cabin door and Ellie opened it right away.

"Glad you could join us."

"So am I." Ruby made a beeline to the couch where Colleen sat and jumped up beside her.

"Hello, girl." She petted her.

"She's a sucker for anyone in distress," he explained.

"And here I thought she just liked me better than you," Colleen said. "It looks like today is our day to see each other."

"So, it does. I hope you don't mind?"

"Not at all."

"Good. Now that we have that established, let's get down to it." Ellie poured a glass of lemonade for Wyatt. "I brought this back from the main house with me and a plate of cookies if you are interested in a snack."

"Don't mind if I do." Wyatt reached for the assortment of Cookie's famous homemade baked goods. "Snickerdoodles."

"I've had two already." Colleen's cheeks pinkened.

"No shame in that," he said.

Ellie cleared her throat. "Colleen, I asked Wyatt to join us because I wanted you to know that you don't only have me, but him supporting you in whatever you say in this session. What happened to you occurred in Chicago and we are in Montana. That's thousands of miles by land and air. You are safe here. We believe you can open up to us and tell us anything and there will not be any repercussions."

"No one is going to find out." Wyatt reached a hand from where he sat in the armchair to cover hers lying on the arm of the couch.

"He said he had connections. He'd always find out. I-I can't risk it."

"Just to be clear, this wasn't the man who attacked you in the lady's room of the Pied Piper?"

"No. He didn't say a word to me."

Ellie scooted to the edge of the chair she sat in. "Can you tell us when this threat was made? How many years ago we're talking?"

"Eight, no, nine years ago."

"So, college?" Wyatt asked.

Colleen nodded.

Ellie wrote this down in her notebook. "Okay. If we proceed this way and ask questions where you either nod or shake your head, then you really won't be speaking the words. Would you agree to doing that? We might be able to guess what happened. And if we can't, we'll stop."

"Okay," Colleen agreed.

Wyatt thought for a moment trying to imagine what could have happened in college that she would have been threatened about and the only thing he could think of made his blood boil. He recalled her having the outburst at the hospital screaming for someone to stop and it made more sense now. Still, he didn't want to jump to that conclusion right away, but he looked Ellie in the eye and he saw she was thinking the same thing. They had to get Colleen to say it for herself, to confirm their suspicions.

"Can I have another cookie?" Colleen asked.

Wyatt reached her the plate and she took two.

"Be careful that Ruby doesn't steal those from you," he warned.

"I will," she assured him, patting Ruby on the head with the hand that didn't hold the cookies. The dog whimpered and laid her head on her bent leg.

"I know we've talked about the eyes until you are sick of it I'm sure, but let's start back there. The eyes and the threat came from when you were in college." Ellie repeated these facts. "Can you tell us why the eyes bother you so much?"

"It's not the eyes as much as what the person was doing that bothers me. I had to stare into those eyes while he did it when he loomed over me."

Colleen stuffed half a cookie in her mouth and chewed fast.

Good God. Did she realize what she had admitted to them?

Wyatt glanced at Ellie and she gave him a slight nod, but held up one finger.

"And where were you when this happened?" Ellie asked in a soft, even voice.

Colleen reached for her lemonade and took a sip. "The basement of his frat house. We weren't alone. Two of his buddies were with him. They held me down while he...while he r-raped me."

As soon as she said the word, she sat the lemonade back on the coffee table and ran from the small living space, down the short hallway to the bathroom. Wyatt started to follow her, but Ellie stopped him.

"I better go."

He sat back down, resting his head in his hands not understanding how she had carried this secret around inside her for over nine years. If she hadn't been attacked at the Pied Piper would she ever have talked about it?

. . .

COLLEEN LOST the contents of her stomach in the commode with Ellie rubbing her back and whispering soothing words. It was Ellie who had come after her and not Wyatt. On one hand she wondered why hadn't he come? And on another she was glad he hadn't. She didn't want him seeing her like this. It was bad enough he'd witnessed her being taken to the hospital after the attack at the Pied Piper.

Ellie flushed the commode and put the lid down. "Take a seat. I'll get you a wet wash cloth."

Tears streamed down her cheeks and she reached for a wad of toilet tissue to blow her nose. Despite her throat being raw from the vomiting, her stomach still roiling, and her emotions raw, she had to say she felt damn good. She felt like a load had been lifted off her chest and her insides had been cleaned out when she threw up. She buried her nose in the tissue and blew before disposing of it in the waste basket. Then she took the wet washcloth that Ellie handed her. She wiped her face all over, and the back of her neck before she wiped her mouth really good.

Shakily, she stood and walked to the sink, cupped her hand under the running faucet and rinsed her mouth out with water. In the vanity mirror, she saw that the color had drained from her face, but a little pink beginning to return to her cheeks.

"I'm proud of you. I can't tell you how proud I am of you, Colleen. You have been so forthcoming in all of our sessions. The assault at the Pied Piper primed you to get this off your chest."

Ellie's kind words made her start crying again, but they weren't sorrowful tears, but happy.

"I feel good. Better than I have in years."

"Good. And we can start work on getting you to the point of feeling even better now. I'll hook you up with a local rape crisis support group where you can go once a week and meet with other survivors while you are here. We'll go into town together and have dinner that evening. No one will have to know what we are doing."

"Thank you, Ellie." Colleen smiled. "You have been so supportive of me."

When Ellie opened the bathroom door, Ruby was sitting there waiting on them. Colleen ruffled the dog's ears before walking back down to the small living area where Wyatt waited, pacing the floor.

He came to her and put his hand on her shoulder, but she leaned into him and he hugged her. "I'm so sorry. I should have picked up on the signs when we were at the hospital. Please forgive me."

"It's okay. We were strangers. How could you be expected to read me?"

"It's my job," he said.

"Forget your job for a moment, Wyatt. Be a human and give yourself some slack. I wasn't ready for anyone to know the truth, not then. Not until we got here."

Ruby whimpered and tried to squeeze in between

them. Wyatt chuckled and stepped back, letting Colleen go. "I can't tell if she is jealous of you or me."

"I think she wanted in on the hug," Ellie observed.

Wyatt and Colleen chuckled, but knelt down and hugged Ruby and the dog licked them both on their cheeks.

CHAPTER 12

COLLEEN WORKED in the stables and with Ellie at her sessions and she felt better every day. She finally learned to ride with Kid's help. And one Saturday afternoon Wyatt took her exploring up in the mountains at the back of the ranch, a true hidden gem that not many clients got to see.

It was hard to believe she'd been at the Brighter Days Ranch almost two weeks, but the evidence was there when she closed her eyes at night and she didn't see those eyes as often. Sometimes, they were still there, but now that Ellie had the sketch they were working on ways to deal with it. They did an exercise where Colleen talked back to the eyes, laughed at the eyes. Ellie even printed out the eyes for Colleen to throw darts at to get her anger out.

Those sessions were exhausting. She'd leave them feeling good, but bone tired. Like this afternoon. All she wanted was to take a shower and take a nap before dinner. She needed it because she had to go to her rape crisis support meeting in Bozeman.

She wasn't watching where she was going as she walked to the main house so, she didn't see Wyatt with his client until she was on them.

"Hey, Colleen," the client said.

Her head jerked up at the sound of the voice and she sucked in her breath. Her eyes felt like they were going to pop out of their sockets and her mouth went dry as she croaked out barely above a whisper, "No. No. Not you." She ran to the main house as fast as she could.

Once inside the main house she fast walked straight to the stair case and took the stairs as quickly as she could, hoping she did not come face to face with anyone. She didn't think she could take having to speak to anyone at the moment. She had to get to the safety of her room and lock the door. She had to separate herself from him. Hadn't Wyatt and Ellie promised her that she was safe here in Montana? That her rapist was in Chicago and it had been when she was in college?

But they didn't know it was Tate Hackles.

Good Lord. How in heaven above had Tate Hackles ended up at the Brighter Days Ranch with her?

Turning the lock on her bedroom door, she sank to the floor and let her breathing return to normal. Slowly breathing in her nose and exhaling out, she repeated this a few times trying to regain control, touching the polished hard pine floor where she sat. Had she made a mistake? It had been nine years since she'd seen the bastard.

Scrambling to her feet, she went over to the partially curtained window and peeked out, trying to see if Wyatt and his client were in view.

"You know Colleen?" Wyatt asked Tate Hackles.

The man shrugged. "I don't know. I said her name so I must, but that was an odd reaction she had, don't you think?"

"Not considering why she's here."

"Is she an ex-soldier too?"

"No." Wyatt walked until they came to the back of the main house and he could look up at the partially drawn curtained window that he'd thought might be Colleen's room a few days ago. Sure, enough he could see her standing there looking out at them. He stood so Hackles' back was to her.

"We've had two good sessions today and were able to take a walk to extend this afternoon's session. I'm pleased with how we've progressed in the last week. How are you feeling about it?"

Hackles put his hands on his hips. "I am too. I was worried at first because of my headaches, but now that they've subsided things are going much more smoothly."

"Yes, they are. And your confusion? How do you feel about it?"

"Good. Not as overwhelmed, until seeing Colleen. I thought she was from my unit or something, but you say she isn't an ex-soldier. Now I don't know how I know her."

"Don't worry. I'm sure you'll figure it out." Wyatt slapped him on his back. "We can't win 'em all, buddy. Let's get you back to your cabin now. We'll pick up tomorrow morning."

"Sure. And maybe I'll remember where I know that girl from."

"Don't stress over it and make yourself get a headache. That is the last thing we want. Let the memories come naturally. Remember what we've been talking about. Like Taz mentioned when we met with him."

"Yeah, it was good to know someone else here has been through what I have and is doing so well. He actually is holding down a real job again."

"He is. Just like I am with my PTSD."

Once they reached the cabin and Hackles was inside, Wyatt jogged back toward the main house. He went inside and was surprised to bump into Ellie coming out of Hannah's office with a stack of freshly printed copies of the artist's sketch.

"What are you going to do with those?" he asked.

"I let Colleen hang these up on a tree trunk and throw darts at them. It helps her release her anger towards her attacker. It's something we learned at the rape crisis support meeting we attended in Bozeman."

"Can I see one of those?"

"Sure." Ellie handed him a page and he swore under his breath. "What is it, Wyatt?"

"I knew when I met Hackles that I had seen him before. I just couldn't put my finger on where." Wyatt shook his head and pointed at the printed paper. "It's the eyes. He's the eyes."

"Are you kidding me?"

"I wouldn't begin to kid about something as serious as this. Colleen ran into us on her way to the main house half an hour ago. She looked petrified when she saw him. Her words were, 'No. No. Not you.' Then she ran into the house. I saw her staring down at us from her bedroom window."

"Damn. But Hackles hasn't a clue, does he?" Ellie scratched her head, pacing the floor.

Wyatt shook his head. "He said 'hey, Colleen', but hasn't the foggiest how he knows her."

"Fuck."

"Ellie Danner!" Hannah entered the front door. "What has you using that kind of language?"

They filled her in on the situation and Hannah sank into the nearest chair. "This is horrible."

Wyatt headed toward the stairs.

"Where you going?" Ellie called.

"To check on Colleen. My original destination when I came into the house."

"Last door on the left."

"Got it." He took the stairs two at a time and was down the decorated hallway in seconds, knocking on the bedroom door.

Colleen opened it, her eyes red from crying. She was also dressed differently than she was earlier and she smelled floral fresh like she'd just stepped out of a shower.

"Go away, Wyatt." She tried to shut the door, but he stopped her, putting his foot in the doorway so it wouldn't close. She glared at him, but didn't open the door wider.

"I think we need to talk."

"What's there to talk about?"

"Why you ran away earlier."

"Isn't it obvious?"

"No."

She flung the door all the way open and stepped into the space until she was almost nose to nose with him because of the boots she was wearing. "Did you have any idea that your client was my rapist?"

"No. I thought I recognized him from somewhere on the first day, but couldn't place him." He pulled her to him and held her close. "The person who attacked you in college is not the man on this ranch."

"How can you say that?" Colleen pushed away from him, breaking free of his embrace.

"Because Tate Hackles suffered a traumatic brain injury in theatre. He's been recovering at Walter Reed hospital in Bethesda for months. He can't remember the simplest tasks; the fact your name came to him out of the blue when he saw you is a mystery he is trying to figure out, but if he thinks too long or too hard on it he will get a headache or possibly a migraine. TBI literally scrambles a person's brain."

"So, you're saying he doesn't remember his past? Even though he knew me upon seeing me, he doesn't remember what he did to me?"

"That's right."

Colleen speared her fingers through her short-cropped hair and paced the room. "This is...this is... awful." She sat on the edge of the bed. "If he can't remember now then it stands to reason he won't ever remember? Right?"

Wyatt nodded, sitting down on the bed, but making sure he gave her space. "The probability of him getting his full memory back is unlikely, but it could happen. Taz has TBI and he did, but it also depends on the severity of the brain injury. I've not had medical training, but I can tell you that Hackles' injury was far more intense than what Taz went through and Taz will tell you the same thing, but we're not telling Hackles that. We're trying to be positive with the man for his therapy. Not giving him false hope, but giving him hope at this point, because anything is possible. It's all in God's hands, after all."

There was a pregnant pause in the room and Wyatt

felt uncomfortable, that maybe he'd lost her for a moment, but then she spoke.

"What are the chances that I finally open up about my assault and I come face to face with him again out here?" She stood up abruptly and started pacing again. "I need to think about this. I need to decide what I want to do. It was one thing being afraid to report it because of being ashamed and afraid of him, because of what he said he'd do if I told. But, now that I've told what happened to me it's all different. The ball is in my court. I'm in control for now. I'm not scared of his threats anymore. I need to face him. I need to know I'm not scared to look him in the eye."

"And do what, Colleen?" Wyatt asked.

"I'll know when I look him in the eye."

"Not today. I think it's too soon for you. Your emotions are too raw. At the same time, I have to consider my client as well. Tate's had a full day of sessions and he needs his rest. I don't want to overload him at this point in his therapy either."

"Tomorrow then?" She asked, studying him hard.

"We'll see. It'll depend on his headache situation. That has controlled his therapy from day to day for the last two weeks."

She shook her head. "Yeah, let's protect the rapist, forget about the victim here."

He didn't like her snarky tone. "Colleen, that's unfair. That's not what I'm doing at all."

"Isn't it? To me it sounds like it."

"Hey, I don't want to be in the middle, but I feel like I am. I'm his therapist and I'm your protector. The fact that he's also your rapist from college ..." Wyatt let his words falter feeling wedged between rocks with no easy way out.

"Chicago doesn't have a statute of limitations; do you know that?" Colleen blurted out. Her lip trembled as she said it.

"No. I didn't."

"I've been doing research in the evenings. They threw it out recently. I could still press charges against him, if I wanted."

Wyatt took a deep breath and let it out slowly, running his right hand up and down the back of his neck. "You have every right to do that, but think long and hard before you make that move. Would it be righting a wrong? Or heaping more coals on a tormented man?"

"What about justice for me?" Colleen asked.

"You have the mental capacity to seek counseling to deal with it and get better. He doesn't. He can go through all the counseling out there but the probability of him getting over this is unlikely."

COLLEEN TURNED her back on Wyatt. She heard what he was saying and although she didn't like it, she got it. Tate Hackles' brain injury was giving him a clean slate, she hoped he didn't screw it up.

"I was a mess after the rape. I know the two aren't the same, but my world was turned upside down afterward just like his is now with the brain injury. And if what you are saying is true then my taking him to court over what happened will not change anything. He's serving a life sentence with the TBI. The criminal justice system couldn't throw more years at him than that."

"That's one way of looking it," Wyatt said. "Thank you for understanding."

Colleen laughed and shook her head. "Don't thank me just yet. I'm not as gracious as I sound, but I'm willing to try and give myself and Hackles some time before moving to charge him. Like you said, he could recover in time."

"It could be years."

"No statute remember."

"Would you seriously spend your time watching him like a hawk to see if he did?"

She shrugged. "All I can think about is what if he tries to assault someone else? How would I live with myself knowing I didn't press charges again him?"

Wyatt blew out a breath he didn't realize he'd been holding. "We have no idea if that is still in his nature."

"Can you tell me what the plan is? Will he be staying at the ranch indefinitely to make sure that if he does regain his memory or if he does begin showing signs of sexual misconduct with the opposite sex that he will be confronted about it?"

"That's something I'll have to talk with Hannah about. She's in charge of his treatment plan, how long he stays. But she doesn't want anyone here put in danger by another client. She'd be the first one to call the authorities on him if she thought he was a threat."

"Thank you." Colleen leaned toward him and kissed him on the cheek.

"For what?" Wyatt asked.

"You knew I needed to come here. You knew what was best for me. You are a good protector, even when put in hard positions."

"I'm glad you feel that way because I had my doubts after bringing you here and Hackles showed up."

"You had no way of knowing he'd be here," Colleen said. "Or that he'd be the client Hannah wanted you to work with when you came."

"I could have taken you away from here as soon as I saw his file and that he had been falsely accused of sexual misconduct twice, but never charged in either case due to lack of evidence. Those records were sealed, but because of the TBI they were unsealed for medical purposes. Yet, Hannah assured me she had a plan in place and Ellie was aware and Taz had my six if it came down to it, but after meeting Hackles it was clear he wasn't functioning on that level. I didn't believe you or any other female was in danger on the ranch."

"Again, it sounds like you were acting in my best interest."

"It still doesn't feel like it knowing what I know now about him."

She smiled at him. "I'm okay."

"I see that." He pushed a lock of hair out of her eyes. "Want to get out of here tonight? Maybe drive into Bozeman for dinner?"

"I'd love to but I already have plans with Ellie. It's our night to go to my rape crisis support meeting in Bozeman. We do dinner. Another time?"

"Sure."

Colleen shoved her hands in her back-jean pockets. "Where's Ruby?"

"Playdate with Emma. She's been pestering Hank according to him since I got back to have one with Ruby so we set one up for today."

"Still not found her a puppy?"

"There's a litter of pups available, but not old enough to be weaned yet. She's going to go pick one out next week."

"That should be fun."

"Yeah. It'll make my moving to Chicago with Ruby easy on her too. Hank said he should make me buy the dog for her for having decided to make the move."

Colleen grinned at him. "Aw, but he loves Emma. I think she has him wrapped around her little finger and he knows it."

"Of course, she does." He stood and moved to leave, but stopped. "You know, I can drive you to Bozeman for your meeting."

"That's sounds great, Wyatt," Ellie said from the doorway. "I was coming to see if I could beg off tonight. Sorry for the late notice, Colleen, but Hannah has a report on that case from last week we were working on that came in today that we have to get turned around pronto."

"What do you say?" Wyatt asked.

"Okay then," Colleen agreed. "I'll be down in five minutes."

CHAPTER 13

THE RESTAURANT in Bozeman Wyatt picked was a steak house which didn't surprise Colleen. Most of the restaurants she'd seen on the drive were steak houses or a variation. But if she'd wanted meat and potatoes they could have eaten on the ranch. Cookie grilled up some of the best steaks' eatable.

She ordered a salad with grilled chicken and ate a little too much yeast bread that was served with it. If Wyatt noticed he didn't mention it.

"You want dessert?" he asked, pushing his finished plate away.

"No. I'm stuffed. I'll need a walk before my meeting."

"Will we have time?" he looked at his watch.

She checked the time on her cell phone and noticed she suddenly had twenty-two missed calls. Rotten reception at the ranch. "I'm sorry. I have several missed calls. I need to see if one of them is from the event planner job I'm waiting to hear back from. Do you mind?"

"No. Go ahead."

She quickly scrolled through and saw they were mostly from pharma reps sending out the latest details on new drugs. One was from her mom, another her dad.

"Nothing. Do you think that is bad?"

"Maybe they are busy with events they are planning which is keeping them from making call backs."

"Wishful thinking I'm sure. I bet I didn't get the job." She sighed. "Which is a bummer because my second interview went great. They said I'd be hearing back from them shortly. I guess I'll continue as a drug rep for a little longer. Something will come up soon."

"You don't know that for sure. Don't sell yourself short. Give them more time to reach out," Wyatt suggested.

They paid for their meals and headed out to take a short walk before Colleen's meeting at the community center. "What does Ellie normally do while you are in your meeting?" Wyatt asked.

"She goes with me as my support person."

"Oh. I don't guess that will work tonight. Wrong gender."

"Exactly. The others wouldn't feel comfortable with you there."

"Don't worry. I'll find something to do while you

are in the meeting. It usually lasts about?"

"An hour. There's a bookstore down this way if you want to hang out in there." Colleen suggested, taking his hand as they walked. "I'm glad you are here with me."

"I am too."

He stopped walking and tilted her chin up, leaning down and brushing his lips across hers. He smiled when she didn't back away from him. "I've wanted to do that since you came down the stairs the other day for lunch."

"Then what took you so long?" she asked.

"I didn't think it was appropriate. You were assaulted. I was assigned to protect you. I shouldn't be making moves on you."

"I'll decide what's right and wrong between us. And I say yes to kissing."

"Is that right?" Wyatt tried not to chuckle as he responded to her, but he couldn't help it. She sure was a contradiction of the situation in his book. "Then I suppose you'll want to go with me to the town dance coming up?"

"I already have my outfit, thanks to Ellie."

"Oh, you do?"

"Yep."

"Remind me to thank her."

Colleen giggled as they began walking and he took her hand again, this time entwining his fingers with hers.

. . .

WYATT LEFT COLLEEN at the community center and circled back to the local bookstore to browse, but found it was getting ready to close for the evening. Most of the stores along the street in the area were shuttered even though it was only seven, so he found a diner and took the last open stool at the counter where he ordered coffee and a piece of pie.

The flat screen television on the wall nearest his end of the counter had CNN news on and he was surprised when he saw coverage of a shooting at a church and then an interview with Commander Burns.

"Pardon me, but can you turn that up?" he asked the waitress.

"Sure hon," she said. "Someone you know? It happened last week in Chicago."

"It did?"

"Yeah, there was even abduction associated with it."

"Damn."

"Apparently this is all connected to some bar getting shot up."

"Yeah, I was working that one."

"You a cop?" she asked, sitting down his pie and topping off his coffee. "Maybe military the way you're dressed in those cargo pants. I see a lot of military types in here dressed that way? Or one of those volunteers?"

"No, private security."

"Hmm. I thought to myself when you walked in that one has a story. Well, if you need anything let me know."

Wyatt cut into his pie, shoving a bite into his mouth, and watched the footage piecing as much as he could together from the clips that were being shown of the week before. He pulled his phone out and checked on the off chance that Burns had called him back from earlier, but no new messages. He hadn't really expected anything after seeing this, but it hadn't hurt to check.

One of his teammates could have reached out to him. They had been silent this whole time preoccupied with their individual assignments. It was so unlike them. Maybe he should take the time to give one of them a call. Communication did go both ways, but which one?

He'd spoken to Will last when Jules and Colleen spoke briefly before they left Chicago. Don Juan called from DC because Simone had been having a panic attack and needed his help talking her through it. He hadn't spoken to Brand since the Saturday after the bar shooting.

Colleen hadn't mentioned if she'd been in touch with her friends either since she left Chicago. But maybe she wanted it that way while she was here so she could focus on her therapy and not have to rehash what happened at the Pied Piper bar with them or have them concerned about her. He got that.

"Would you like another piece of pie?" the waitress asked, refilling his coffee cup.

"Sure. Make it blueberry this time."

"With whip crème on top?

"Is there any other way to eat it?"

The waitress chuckled, removing his plate to get him another piece of pie. She returned a few moments later with his blueberry with a generous amount of canned whip crème piled on top.

"I haven't seen you around here before," she said.

"I'm out of Eagle Rock. In town with a friend who's at the community center tonight."

"Oh. Well. Glad to have you. I have a cousin who lives in Eagle Rock. Nice little town."

The waitress wandered back toward the other end of the counter to wait on someone else and he noticed the news station had recycled coverage and was reshowing the shooting footage at the church in Chicago before moving on to the SUV explosion in the parking lot and then the interview with Burns.

Wyatt punched Don Juan's number in his address book and it rang a few times before he answered.

"Man, where in hell are you? You're missing all the action out here."

"I told you I was going to Montana the last time we talked."

"Yeah, I know, but still, you should be here. Brand's been injured. The shrapnel in his chest has dislodged and now he needs to have surgery which means he could be given a clean bill of health."

"No! You're shitting me? That's what he's been wanting for so long. Listen, CNN has Chicago all over their coverage right now. What's going on with that? It's over a week old, has something new happened?"

"Yeah, one of the detectives that Burns assigned to drive Carly and Brand around turned out to be a bad egg. He actually knew her ex-husband Porter and he tried to make the shooting at the church look like it was the Twin Cobras coming after her and then he blew up the SUV they were riding in moments later. And to top it off, Carly was abducted the following day."

"What? How could that happen? Brand is stellar at his job."

"Remember I said he was injured. He was in the hospital. And she was abducted by the detective who'd been assigned to drive them, so he was someone she trusted to be around her. It's all over now. She's fine. Brand's been released until he decides if and when he wants to have the surgery."

"Of course, he'll have the surgery. It's a no brainer."

"To you, me, and everyone else it is, but he says he doesn't want to have it. He doesn't want to go back to the SEALS."

"That's crazy."

"Not necessarily. He's met someone."

"He has? How'd he do that? He's been on the job.

When did he have time to…you aren't suggesting that Mr. JOB has broken his rule and got involved with his assignment?"

Don Juan laughed.

"Well, we're all human."

Don Juan laughed even harder at that. When he sobered he asked, "Are you saying you are guilty as well, Mr. Kincaid?"

"Maybe."

"Maybe?"

Wyatt heard the mirth in his pal's voice.

Don Juan's next words were muffled as if he had covered the phone with his hand. "Hey Simone, guess what. I think Colleen has a man."

"Woo Hoo! About damn time she got one."

"I heard her loud and clear tell her," Wyatt said. "But don't go getting all excited we are in the first stages of things."

"First, second, you are there. Better run. She's making eyes at me now."

"Is that good or bad?"

"With her it can be both."

Wyatt ended the call and finished the last of his pie. He drained his coffee cup before the waitress could come back and refill it again. Then he lay a ten beside the plate to cover the bill and tip.

He took his time walking back to the community center to wait for Colleen, not certain he wanted to tell her about Carly, but if the television was on at the ranch she'd see the coverage on Chicago there and he'd rather her hear it from him than someone else.

"What's wrong?" she asked as soon as she saw him.

"There's been a few developments back in Chicago with the Pied Piper case. It's made national news. I saw it when I went into the local diner to wait for you after the book store closed."

"Oh. Okay. Anything I need to be concerned about?"

He nodded. "Carly was abducted, but she has been found and is safe at home again. I was talking to Don Juan because her protector Brand was injured. But everyone is supposed to be okay now."

"Then that is all that matters. Right? I can't make what happened back there go away so I shouldn't let it affect me. I care about my friends and what happens to them, but I have to take care of myself right now. I'm the main concern at the moment. If that sounds selfish then it has to be that way while I recuperate." Her voice was very monotone as she spoke and she refrained from making eye contact with him until she finished.

"Do you really mean that?" he asked.

She shook her head. "I wasn't convincing, was I?"

"No, but you gave it a good try."

"That is what we went over in session tonight. Putting ourselves first. Taking care of ourselves and letting others go because we have been hurt and we have to realize we need to heal before we can be whole again."

"What about letting others take care of you?" he asked.

"We're learning to be strong women, but I think on a case by case basis we could let someone take care of us if it is for the right reason," Colleen tilted her head and smiled at him, hopeful.

He held out his hand and she put hers in his as they started walking back to where he'd parked his truck. "Good because I've wanted to take care of you since I saw you, Colleen Summers."

"Wow, Wyatt, I had to look atrocious."

"Looks had nothing to do with it. I believe we made a connection."

"Are you sure it wasn't the need to get me away from my parents?"

He laughed and shook his head. "There is that."

"I've not been able to have a serious relationship because of what happened to me in college. I've dated a few men now and again over the years, but it was never more than one or two dates, anything more than that and they wanted more from me than I could give them."

"I'm looking for forever, Colleen. If you think you'd like to look for it with me, then let's give it a try. Too many people rush into the physical without getting to know one another."

She smiled at him. "You are an exceptional man, Wyatt Kincaid."

EPILOGUE

WYATT'S PHONE rang as soon as he walked into the main house for breakfast with Colleen the next morning. He answered it on the second ring because it was Commander Burns calling him.

"Hello?"

"Wyatt. Burns here. Sorry I couldn't get back to you sooner, the last week has been hell around here."

"I just saw on CNN last night. I talked to Donovan and he filled me in on most of the details."

"Yeah, the Pied Piper case has imploded. Between what was going on with Carly, then Donovan and Simone taking off to Washington D.C. for the week in search for her father I at least felt she was safe out of town but she wasn't."

"No? Don Juan didn't mention that."

Burns let out a deep breath. "I don't guess he said anything about Jules being abducted either?"

Wyatt grunted. "All he told me was that Brand got injured and could have surgery to get the shrapnel removed so he could go back to the SEALs if he wanted and that Carly was safe."

"She is now that her father, ex-husband, and one of my detectives are all behind bars. The judge denied bail to all three of them. I've never seen that happen before, but she was not buying into their attorney's pleas."

There was a brief silence before Burns spoke again. "I haven't forgotten Colleen or her part of the case. In fact, we finally got a match off that print we lifted from her purse. Her assailant was arrested last night and is in holding as we speak. I just need to know the two of you can be on the next flight out?"

Wyatt sat down on the sofa with a thud. It was like his legs had been pulled out from under him. "You found her attacker?"

"You sound surprised."

"I-I guess I am. The last time we spoke you didn't give much hope in that happening. At least, that is how I took it."

"At the time I didn't believe it would happen either, but as the search narrowed it started looking more promising. And it turns out this guy is wanted on several other assaults so if we can get Colleen to identify him we can put him away for life I believe."

"I want you to be the one to tell Colleen. She just came downstairs for breakfast. Let me get her," Wyatt said. He motioned to her at the stairs to come join him.

"What is it?" she asked. "Who's on the phone?"

"Commander Burns. He's got something to tell you." Wyatt handed her the phone and she put it up to her ear.

"Hello?"

"Colleen, how are you today?"

"Intrigued, but good. How are things in Chicago?"

"Crazy right now, but I am pleased to tell you that we have your man behind bars. We found him from the print we lifted off your purse and all I need is for you to come back and identify him."

"But what if I can't? I didn't see him, Commander."

"But you gave us that sketch."

"Of my rapist from when I was in college. The eyes, belonged to him. Didn't Wyatt talk to you about that? In my dazed state my mind gave you a memory from my past."

There was a long pause. "He called, left a message about needing to talk to me, but I've been so busy I'm just now getting back to him. When we talked I caught him up on what was going on here and that we'd caught your attacker. I didn't give him the chance to tell me why he'd originally called. I assume you've been dealing with all of these emotions old and new while in Montana?"

"I have. I have faced my demons and getting the help I need."

"Glad to hear it. So when can I expect you and Wyatt in Chicago?"

"As soon as I talk to my counselor here and we can make arrangements to leave. Wyatt also has a client here that he may not be able to leave just yet, but I'll let him deal with that."

Colleen handed the phone back to Wyatt and went to Hannah's office door which was closed, she knocked once then twice before it opened.

"Good morning, Colleen. Is there something I can do for you?" Hannah asked.

"I need to reach Ellie and let her know I'm needed back in Chicago right away to identify my attacker at the Pied Piper Bar. I also need to know if she feels I need to return to the ranch or if I found a support group in Chicago to continue group sessions with if that would work."

"That's wonderful that they caught him. Ellie had to drive into Eagle Rock to pick up some supplies for the ranch first thing this morning, but I'll be sure to let her know you are looking for her when she gets back." Hannah leaned against the door frame staring at Wyatt. "I guess if you are leaving he'll be going too?"

"I don't know. Depends on how badly Hackles needs him here."

"He needs him, but Wyatt has a job in Chicago waiting for him. I knew that when he came here. Let's go look at flights for you both out of Bozeman," Hannah said. "Cole Ramsey will be back next week earlier than expected. He called last night to inform me of his impending return. Ellie will be freed up and she can do a few sessions with Hackles until Cole gets here and then he can take him on permanent. It'll work out. These things always do."

Wyatt wandered into the office a few minutes later once he ended his phone call and wrapped his arm around Colleen's waist. "What are we doing?"

"Looking for flights to Chicago. The cheapest out of Bozeman with no layovers is at six a.m. tomorrow."

"We don't need a flight."

"We don't?" Colleen looked at him surprised.

"A Senator Wills who is the father of a former sorority sister of yours is in Bozeman right now and he has offered to give us a lift back to Chicago. Apparently Burns is friends with him and was able to pull a few strings for us."

"Margot Wills!" Colleen bounced on the balls of her feet. "I haven't seen her since graduation."

Wyatt nodded. "So you do know her?"

"Of course. If you think Simone is a handful, wait until you meet Margot."

"You're kidding right?

Colleen shook her head.

"That girl has a T at the end of her name for a reason and it spells trouble."

Hannah laughed. "Sounds like she might need a Brotherhood Protector of her own."

ALSO BY LEANNE TYLER

Enjoy other Brotherhood Protector books by Leanne Tyler:

ABOUT LEANNE TYLER

Award-winning author Leanne Tyler writes sweet and somewhat sensual romances whether historical, contemporary, or romantic suspense. Her newest series the Chicago Protection Task Force is part of the Brotherhood Protection World. Other series includes her popular The Good Luck series--a collection of short contemporary romantic comedy romances set in East Tennessee. In addition to her contemporary novels, she writes American historical novels set prior to and during the Civil War.

Leanne lives in East Tennessee with her son and newest addition, a 2 ½ year old yorkie maltese mix named Willie. For more information about her books and to sign up for her newsletter, please visit leannetyler.com.

BROTHERHOOD PROTECTORS

ORIGINAL SERIES BY ELLE JAMES

ABOUT ELLE JAMES

ELLE JAMES also writing as MYLA JACKSON is a *New York Times* and *USA Today* Bestselling author of books including cowboys, intrigues and paranormal adventures that keep her readers on the edges of their seats. With over eighty works in a variety of sub-genres and lengths she has published with Harlequin, Samhain, Ellora's Cave, Kensington, Cleis Press, and Avon. When she's not at her computer, she's traveling, snow skiing, boating, or riding her ATV, dreaming up new stories. Learn more about Elle James at www.elle-james.com

Website | Facebook | Twitter | GoodReads | Newsletter | BookBub | Amazon

Follow Elle!
www.ellejames.com
ellejames@ellejames.com

facebook.com/ellejamesauthor
twitter.com/ElleJamesAuthor